Lethal Legacy

Other Avalon Books by S. R. Hawley

DESERT GOLD
DEADLY SECRETS

LETHAL LEGACY

S.R. HAWLEY

AVALON BOOKS
THOMAS BOUREGY AND COMPANY, INC.
401 LAFAYETTE STREET
NEW YORK, NEW YORK 10003

Library of Congress Catalog Card Number: 91-75755
ISBN 0-8034-8906-4

PRINTED IN THE UNITED STATES OF AMERICA
ON ACID-FREE PAPER
BY HADDON CRAFTSMEN, SCRANTON, PENNSYLVANIA

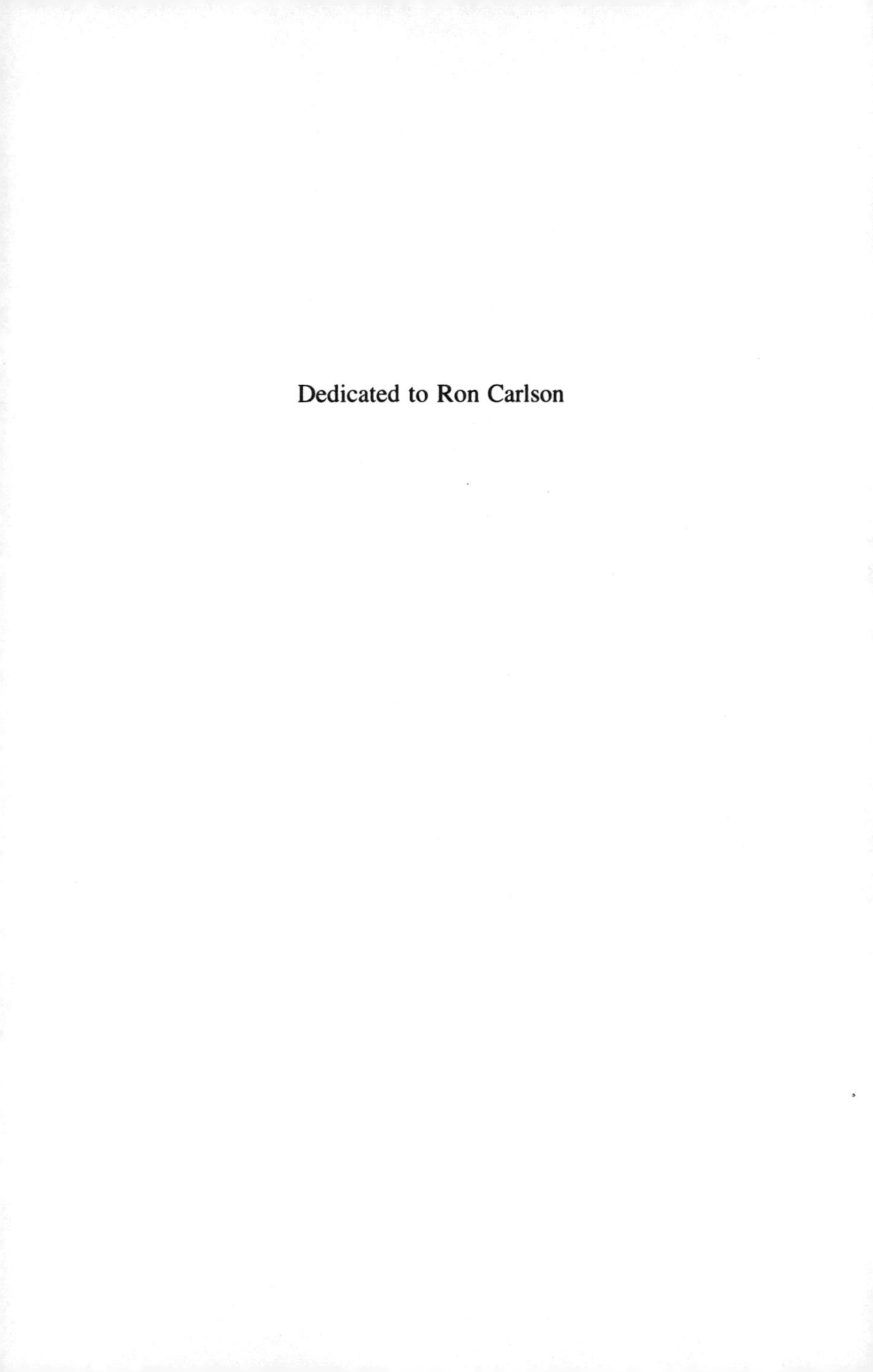

Dedicated to Ron Carlson

Chapter One

Rebecca Brown absentmindedly tore leaves from the head of lettuce and dropped them into the salad spinner. The big, round clock on the back kitchen wall was nearing five o'clock. She sighed loudly, realizing that time was running out, snapped the lid on the spinner, and gave the handle a good crank.

It was almost too late to expect a call. She glanced again at the clock to reassure herself of the remaining time. After a year of teaching second grade, she had almost forgotten the misery of job hunting. With three months of summer recess facing her, however, and only one month's pay saved, she was again becoming familiar with the ego-bashing that accompanied a job search.

She popped the top off the spinner and munched thoughtfully on a piece of crisp lettuce. Her major obstacle to landing a job was thc timc framc. Most employers didn't want to hire someone for only three months. Mr. Flemming at Sound City, though, had been looking for a summertime bookkeeper.

Her previous banking experience had put her in the running, and Flemming had told her that he'd let her know by Friday afternoon.

Rebecca felt her chances diminishing with each turn of the clock's second hand. In an attempt to save money, she had turned off her air conditioner, despite the heat wave blanketing southern California. A small fan on the kitchen counter oscillated slowly back and forth, barely stirring the warm air in her apartment.

Cool salad in hand, she crossed into the living room and plopped heavily onto the sofa. She eyed the phone on the end table for a moment, as though by force of will she might make it ring, then glanced again at the indicator light on the answering machine, still slightly disbelieving that no one had called her while she'd been out putting in applications. The red light shone back at her like an unblinking eye—no messages.

She munched a bit of salad and enjoyed a short respite from the heat as the fan tilted momentarily in her direction, gently caressing her cheek and lightly tufting her long, blond hair. As five o'clock drew ever nearer, she maintained a stubborn hope that Flemming would call.

Maybe, she thought, he had simply misplaced her number and was at this very moment searching frantically for it through the stacks of paper on his desk. Or maybe he'd asked his secretary to call and she'd forgotten.

Rebecca smiled cynically at her own daydreams. No, she realized, she simply hadn't been hired. The fan made another brief pause in her direction, and she turned to glimpse a patch of bright-blue sky through the open arcadia door that led to the balcony of her third-floor apartment. A row of green plants in multicolored pots were perched on the pink railing.

The cheery scenery couldn't lift her falling spirits, however. She had honestly believed that she would land the job at Sound City. She was certainly qualified, if not exactly current.

She had put her two years of employment at SoCal Bank to good use, becoming expert on ten-key and encoding machines. Further, she had studied business at Cal State Fullerton for two years.

In fact, until her junior year at college she had intended to become an accountant. But the impersonal nature of the business school had gradually chipped away at her enthusiasm, and one day she had realized that the cold world of business simply wasn't for her. She had changed her major to liberal arts and two years later had earned an elementary-teaching certificate.

She picked at the salad with her fingers. Maybe teaching hadn't been such a good choice, after all. The hope she had been holding for the job at Sound City was quickly turning to despair and anger.

Well, she thought, if Flemming didn't want her, that was his loss. There were other places that would hire her. She had put out six applications today; one of them would call. And if they didn't, she would put out six more. Los Angeles was a job hunter's dream. The classified section in the *Times* was as thick, or thicker, than the entire newspaper in some smaller cities. And most of those jobs paid more than the one at Sound City, anyway.

Suddenly Rebecca stopped and smiled to herself. She was getting worked up over nothing. It was only a summer job she wanted. Come September, she would be back in the friendly confines of her second-grade classroom at McDill Elementary School.

With a sigh of resignation, she turned for the TV remote

on the table beside the phone. Monday would start a new week. Until then, she thought, she may as well enjoy her free time.

Suddenly the phone rang.

She was so surprised by the unexpected sound that she almost jumped. She glanced quickly at the timer on her VCR. It was just after five. Could it be Flemming?

A wave of hope surged through her. Fighting the urge to yank the phone to her ear and immediately accept the position, Rebecca allowed it to ring a second time. It wouldn't do, she thought, to pounce on the phone as though she had been waiting for the call. She smiled wryly, even though she had been. For whatever his reasons, Flemming had waited this long to contact her, and another ring or two couldn't hurt.

The phone rang again. Rebecca lifted the receiver, feeling hopeful expectation. "Hello," she said, hoping to hear Flemming's voice in return.

"Rebecca Brown?" a well-modulated man's voice asked. It wasn't Flemming's.

"Speaking," she said. She had been hoping to hear about a job; now she was certain she would be listening to a telephone solicitor's spiel.

"My name is Delbert Tipton," the man said. "I'm with Four Points Investigations in Tucson, Arizona."

He paused dramatically, evidently waiting for Rebecca to respond. But she was barely listening. Finally he continued. "I've been searching for you for some time," he said.

Suddenly she was listening very carefully. "Searching?" she asked, her suspicions raised. "For me?"

Tipton came right to the point. ''I have some information,'' he said, ''about your father.''

She was immediately skeptical. ''My father,'' she began haltingly. ''My father and my mother . . . both were killed in an automobile accident five years ago.''

Tipton allowed no time for sympathy. ''I'm not talking about your adoptive parents,'' he said.

Rebecca was momentarily dumbstruck. ''My father?'' she asked, not realizing that she was speaking.

''Your natural father,'' Tipton corrected.

''What kind of information?'' Rebecca asked, beginning to regain her composure.

''His name,'' Tipton said bluntly.

Rebecca bit her lip. Her heart was pounding so loudly that she was certain Tipton must hear it over the phone. She had once started a search for her natural parents, but mounds of bureaucratic red tape had put an end to it. Still, she had never stopped wondering who her true parents were.

Tipton filled the silence on the line. ''I need to meet with you,'' he said.

Rebecca's thoughts were a jumble. ''How could you know that?'' she asked.

''Don't worry about how; just be certain that I do,'' Tipton answered, his voice smooth and flat. ''I've been hired to find you. I've done that. I could leave now and still receive my pay.''

''Leave?'' Rebecca's voice was despairing. ''Why would you leave?''

''Listen carefully,'' Tipton said. His tone was as flat and unemotional as a computer voice chip. ''For you, this is a family matter. For me, it's business. I was hired to locate you, and that's what I'll be paid for.'' He coughed over the phone. ''There's more to it, but nothing that I can discuss with you over the phone.''

''Can you at least tell me his name?'' Rebecca asked.

''The only way you'll learn that is to take a trip with me.''

''A trip? Where?'' Despite her suspicions, Rebecca did not slam down the phone. The possibility of learning her father's identity kept her on the line.

''Again, you've asked a question I can't answer.''

''Just a minute,'' she said, trying to gain control of the conversation. ''I don't even know who you are.''

''Do you know about August fifth?'' Tipton asked.

The question struck from nowhere with the force of a solid punch. August 5, her true date of birth, had been accidentally transposed as August 3 on the birth certificate issued with her adoption. Somehow someone somewhere had located the mistake and informed her parents. She had celebrated her seventh birthday twice that year, once on the third, to say good-bye to the old date, and again on the fifth, to welcome in the new. Very few people knew about this.

''You know about my birthday?'' she asked quietly, not quite believing it was possible.

Tipton's voice lost, for the moment, its mechanical monotone. ''If you'd like to learn about your father,'' he urged, ''you'll have to come with me.''

''Where?'' Rebecca asked, forgetting she'd already put forth the question. A dead line was her response. ''Can you at least tell me how long?'' she asked.

He resumed his business voice. "Two days," he said. "We leave tonight. You'll be back Sunday afternoon."

Rebecca quickly mulled over the situation. She could always accept the offer, then back out later. "All right," she said. "I'll go."

"Good." Tipton sounded as if he'd said it merely because it was expected. "I'm at the Wave's Crest Motel." He quickly outlined directions for finding it. Rebecca scribbled quickly on the pad beside her phone, noting that the motel was located in a particularly seedy section of LA.

"Meet me at ten-thirty," he said.

Considering the location of the motel and the late hour at which he wanted to meet, Rebecca tried for another time. "I don't know if I can make it tonight," she hedged.

"Then you won't make it at all," Tipton responded. "It's tonight or never. We're racing a deadline. Make up your mind."

His pushy manner was aggravating, but Rebecca was determined not to allow Tipton to drag her into a dangerous meeting in downtown. "I'm going to call the police before I leave," she told him. "I'm going to tell them everything about this conversation. I'm also going to call the police when I arrive. I may want them to escort me to your room."

"Fine," Tipton said. "Let me give you my Tucson phone number." He read it to her. "Call and ask my secretary about case number 9109BR. Call as soon as I hang up. She doesn't like to stay late, and she usually leaves about this time. Make sure to identify yourself and read her the case number. She'll be able to tell you everything I've just told you, but nothing more. I realize you must have doubts, but let me assure you this case is for real."

Rebecca could sense that he was telling the truth, but she refused to drop her guard. "I'll make the call," she said. "And if it checks out, I'll meet you at ten-thirty, with a policeman at my side."

"Bring the entire cavalry," he answered. "Just be there."

The Wave's Crest Motel was a dilapidated, two-story, L-shaped building just beyond the boundary of Little Tokyo. Rebecca lurched in her seat as the car bounced over one of the potholes littering the parking lot. Vance Foster, who was driving, grimaced at the jolt. "Didn't see that one," he said.

Rebecca checked her watch. They were five minutes early. She surveyed the parking lot. A row of cars were parked nose-in toward the building along a sidewalk that fronted the motel; otherwise the lot was empty.

Vance eased his car slowly along the motel's front, squinting his eyes against the darkness, trying to read the numbers on the room doors. Unable to see the doors from the passenger seat, Rebecca watched him, waiting for the look of recognition that would signal he'd found the room.

As soon as she'd hung up with Tipton, she'd dialed the number he'd given her. Her call had been answered by a prerecorded message announcing that Four Points Investigations was closed for the day and instructing her to leave a message at the sound of the tone.

Beginning to wonder if Tipton really did work for a detective agency, she'd called directory assistance in Arizona and asked for a listing for Four Points. When the operator had read back to her the same number Tipton had given, her suspicions were somewhat allayed. Still, the fact that Four Points Investigations existed didn't necessarily mean that Tipton was an employee. He might simply have taken the name and number from an Arizona phone book.

"Should be coming up any minute," Vance said, still peering at the doors. The car crawled slowly forward. "There it is." He nodded vaguely at a red door in a row of identical red doors.

Vance wasn't a policeman; he was the principal at McDill Elementary. Afraid that the police would simply laugh at her request for an escort to the motel, Rebecca had called Vance and explained the situation to him.

She hadn't had to ask him to come; he had insisted. Rebecca smiled to herself. Vance had always gone out of his way to lend her a hand. He was a close friend and one of the few who knew that she was adopted.

Not that she was ashamed of her adoption, but she considered it a personal matter. She wasn't comfortable discussing it except with those she trusted as her friends. Vance even knew about the mix-up with her birthdays.

He was an older man, nearing retirement age, and a bit stocky, with a head of thick, wavy gray hair and a wide smile permanently affixed to his fatherly face. He and his wife were childless, to their great disappointment, and Rebecca knew that Vance took a great deal of satisfaction from his job as principal because it meant he was always surrounded by children.

He parked the car and nodded at her. "Well," he said, "let's find out what's what."

Rebecca smiled weakly. She was suddenly nervous and frightened. She had suspected a setup of some kind from the start. Now every shadow seemed to hold a sinister secret.

Vance was climbing from the car. Despite his smile, she could tell he was nervous. If anything happened to him, she would never forgive herself.

"Wait," she called out, not moving from her seat. Vance turned and faced her through the open driver's door. "Maybe we should just turn around and go home," she said.

Vance laughed, just a little too loudly, Rebecca thought. "Turn around?" he asked. "After all the convincing I had to do with my wife to allow me to drive you to a motel in the middle of the night?"

She met his eyes. "It's too dark. I don't like the looks of this."

He turned from the car. "It's just a motel," she heard him say. "People pull in every night." Then he turned back to her. "This could be your only chance." He circled the car and opened her door. "Nothing's going to happen. You're going to meet Tipton, and then we'll decide if you should travel with him."

They walked along the sidewalk to Tipton's door in silence. "Here we are," Vance said. He rapped on the metal door.

It swung open several inches.

Rebecca stepped back, behind Vance.

He glanced at her over his shoulder. This time she could see the strain in his smile. "A little strange," he said.

The door opened into a wedge of blackness. Vance pushed the door in farther with the tip of his finger. The room was as silent as it was dark.

"Anyone home?" Vance called. "Tipton?"

The pale light that trickled through the open doorway revealed a dark-green carpet. Rebecca peered into the room and could make out the dark silhouettes of the bed, a chair, and a long, low chest of drawers.

Vance fumbled inside the doorway for a switch, and the room was suddenly alight. "Tipton?" he called again.

"Let's go," Rebecca urged. The phone call, the demand for a meeting at this seedy motel, and now the broken appointment. The entire situation seemed too strange and filled with danger. "We can come back in the morning."

Vance stepped inside the room. "Just a quick look around," he said. "Maybe he just stepped out for a minute." He crossed toward the bed.

Feeling suddenly alone and vulnerable on the sidewalk, Rebecca followed him in. "We should wait outside," she told him.

Vance wasn't listening, though. He had circled the bed and was staring at the floor. "Would you look at that?" he said.

"What?" Rebecca asked sharply. She quickly crossed to his side. A suitcase lay open on the floor, its contents strewn about in a confused jumble.

Vance crouched and absently slid his fingers through some of the clothing. "It's men's," he said, more to himself than Rebecca.

Suddenly he stood up and turned to the shallow alcove that led to the closed bathroom door.

Rebecca followed his eyes and was suddenly very scared. "Don't," she begged. "Let's get out of here. We can call the police."

Vance glanced at her. His permanent smile had disappeared. He gripped the knob on the bathroom door. Rebecca's mouth was dry. Her palms were moist. She pressed herself tightly to Vance's back, her hands clinging to his broad shoulders, afraid of what they would find before the door was even opened.

Vance turned the knob and pushed gently against the door. It swung open soundlessly. His hand eased in and flipped the light switch.

Rebecca let out a short scream. Vance spun quickly, and she buried her face in his chest. Then he was hurrying her quickly from the room, her eyes closed, trying to erase the horror she had just seen: a blue-suited man, crumpled in the shower stall, a bullet hole in his head.

Chapter Two

Detective Penning shook his head and rolled his eyes with a look that perfectly expressed his doomed acceptance of bungling. "Let's try it one more time," he said, shifting his glance from Rebecca to Vance. "You first. And it might go a lot faster if you begin by telling me all of the things in that room that you *didn't* touch."

Vance cleared his throat nervously. He and Rebecca had twice begun to tell their story and had twice been interrupted by Penning, who seemed to feel it was his duty not only to investigate the crime, but to point out every mistake Vance and Rebecca had made and explain in detail how those mistakes would undoubtedly hamper a speedy resolution of the case.

They were standing on the sidewalk outside the room, inside an area cordoned off by a wide yellow ribbon that marked the crime scene. A small army of investigators had appeared, some wearing orange jumpsuits and carrying black satchels, others dressed in suits and carrying cameras and more black satchels. A contingent of uniformed officers worked the perimeter, keeping a growing crowd of curious sightseers beyond the borders of the yellow ribbon.

Vance again began his story. This time Penning listened to him without interruption, occasionally making a notation in a small spiral-bound notebook he was holding.

When Vance had finished, Penning said, "So you waltzed in, touched everything you could possibly get your hands on, and when you found the body, you grabbed the nearest phone, which just happened to be the phone in the room, and called the police, right?"

"We knocked first," Vance corrected.

Penning thrust out his lower lip, closed his eyes, and nodded his head quickly, searching for the proper words to convey his displeasure. "That makes it all right, then, right?" he asked sarcastically. "First you knocked, then you waltzed in, touched everything you could possibly get your hands on, and when you found the body. . . . Well, you know the rest."

His gaze shifted to Rebecca. "Now, is there anything we've left out of our little reconstruction?"

Though she was sorry for disturbing the crime scene, Rebecca was growing tired of Penning's unending tirade. He was making *them* sound like criminals.

"The door was unlocked," she said defensively. "We had an appointment to meet Delbert Tipton."

Penning fixed her with a long, expressionless stare. "Right," he said at last, flipping his notebook closed. Just then a man wearing an identification card from the medical examiner's office approached the detective.

"What have you got, Doc?" he asked.

"Looks like a .38," the ME responded. "Someone capped him right there in the shower."

"And didn't even get his hair wet," Penning said with a laugh. "He's yours as soon as we're finished here."

Murder was obviously an everyday ritual for the ME, who simply nodded and told Penning that he'd be waiting in his van.

Penning faced the two. "There are prints everywhere," he said. "Of course, half of them are probably yours. We're going to have to bring you downtown to be printed." He narrowed his eyes and shook his head. "If we're lucky, we'll get everything sorted out by Christmas."

Rebecca listened dejectedly. Their actions could have obliterated the one clue that would lead the police to the killer. Of course, they hadn't known that a crime had been committed when they'd entered, but they should have left as soon as they'd discovered the ransacked suitcase. She considered apologizing, but the look on Penning's face convinced her to remain silent.

Suddenly a uniformed officer exited the room and hurried over to Penning, waving two multicolored envelopes in his hands. He handed them to the detective. "Plane tickets," he said. "One for the victim and one for Rebecca Brown."

Penning accepted the tickets with a grunt. "Where were they?" he asked.

"Found them," the officer said. "Suitcase had a false bottom. It was a pretty good one."

"But you managed to spot it?"

The officer smiled, obviously pleased with himself. "That's right."

Penning almost smiled himself. "Good work, Molloy. Anything else?"

"A couple of cigarettes in the ashtray, lipstick on them."

"Had himself a honey, did he?" Penning asked absently. "See what else you can find." He flipped open the envelopes and glanced quickly at the tickets. Rebecca fought the urge to lean forward and check out the destination.

"Well, well," he said at last. "These must be for that trip you were telling me about." He pulled one free of its envelope and scrutinized it. "This is yours," he said, nodding at Rebecca. He eyed the ticket once again. "Who do you know in Phoenix?" he asked.

"Phoenix?" she repeated, her mind already racing.

"That's the place." Penning's eyes bored into her.

"No one," she said quickly. "But that must be where my father is." She could barely contain her excitement.

"Uh-huh." Penning's voice, as usual, betrayed no hint of his thoughts. He glanced at his watch. "Your flight is leaving in thirty minutes. I don't think you're going to make it." Noting her expression, he said, "These tickets are evidence; you wouldn't be able to use them even if they were yours." He signaled a uniformed officer, who approached languidly.

"Hope I'm not disturbing you," Penning said brusquely, pushing the tickets at the officer. "Take care of these."

He returned his attention to Vance and Rebecca. "Whoever killed him made a quick search, and not a very thorough one. They were obviously in a hurry—just turned out his pockets and dug through his suitcase. Got his money, though. Left his empty wallet behind."

He glanced at his notebook. "This Tipton probably came out here to get you and got a little lonely for some company. It just so happens that he found the wrong kind."

Rebecca shuddered.

Penning shrugged. "I'm only guessing, of course. But this sort of thing happens all the time." He closed his notebook. "You're going to have to come downtown and make a statement. And, like I said, we'll want to take your prints. That is, if you don't mind." His voice held the faintest trace of accusation.

"Why would we mind?" Rebecca asked.

"Good question," Penning responded.

"You're not accusing us?" she asked incredulously.

"If I were accusing you, you wouldn't be standing here talking; you'd be in the back of the squad car in cuffs." He turned and walked toward the open door of Tipton's room. "Wait right here," he ordered.

"As if we'd try to make a break for it," Vance muttered under his breath.

Rebecca glanced at him. He looked stooped, tired, and shaken. "I'm so sorry I involved you in this," she said. "It was bad enough that I asked you to drive me out here at night, but now this. . . ." She shrugged helplessly, unable to find words.

Vance smiled at her. "Relax. I was glad to give you a hand when you needed it."

"But now you'll be up all night, and we're involved in this murder. . . ."

"We're not involved in anything," he said. He looked in the direction of the open doorway, then returned his gaze to Rebecca. ''We discovered a body, that's all. Someone was going to find him. We just happened to be the unlucky ones. Anyway, to tell you the truth, I'm finding the whole thing rather exciting. Like watching a movie.''

Rebecca shuddered. ''I just keep thinking of him lying there, his head and shoulders propped up against the wall.'' She shook her head, trying to erase the terrible memory.

Vance nodded. ''I wish you hadn't seen that,'' he said, then quickly changed the subject. ''Do you intend to follow up on this thing and travel to Phoenix?''

She nodded. ''You can't know what it's like, not knowing who your mother and father are. For so long I've resisted the urge to find them. The one time I tried, all I got for my effort was a mountain of red tape and a wall of silence.'' She was momentarily silent, watching a crowd of investigators gather at the motel room door. ''Now I have a clue at least. My father might be in Phoenix. I have to go and find out.''

Vance laid a reassuring hand on her shoulder. ''If you need anything, money or anything else, just ask. You know I'll do whatever I can.''

Rebecca felt a blush of embarrassment. ''Thank you,'' she said, averting her gaze. ''I've managed to save some money, and now that school's out, I have nothing but time. With a little luck, I'll find some answers in Phoenix.''

Detective Penning returned with a uniformed officer. ''Well, it's pretty clear,'' he reported. ''Someone backed

Tipton into the john, popped him in front of the shower, took the money, and ran."

Rebecca felt her stomach lurch at his matter-of-fact manner.

"All we have to do now is find out who did it," he continued. He jerked his head in the direction of the uniformed officer. "This is Officer Brody. He'll drive you downtown, take your statements, and have you fingerprinted."

Brody faced the pair impassively.

Penning faced Vance. "We'll find someone else to drive your car to the station. When you're finished with your statements, you'll be free to leave."

"I'll want to call my wife," Vance said. "I don't want her worrying."

"Sure, sure." Penning nodded. "Down at the station." As an afterthought he added, "I'm surprised you didn't call her from the room." He laughed quietly to himself and said, "I guess miracles do happen." Then he turned his back on them and left.

"Over there," Brody said, pointing to a squad car parked at the curb.

The three headed to police headquarters.

Chapter Three

Rebecca sat on the edge of the bed, took a deep breath, and prepared herself to make the call. She caught a glimpse of sunlight and blue Arizona sky through the window of her room on the second floor of the Painted Sands Motel. She wondered how Philip would react. They hadn't seen each other in over three years, and now here she was, not only calling, but asking for a favor as well.

She lay back on the bed for a moment and stared at the ceiling, trying to gather her courage. She had arrived in Phoenix on Monday morning and had discovered within two days that all agencies concerned with adoption were as tight-lipped as she had remembered them to be.

She wished she knew how private investigators uncovered their information. Probably a network of informants, she guessed.

The thought helped calm her nerves slightly. If private investigators could use sources to track down information, so could she. She sat up and eyed the name she'd scribbled on the tablet that rested beside her on the bed: Philip Grant.

A scrollwork of nervous doodlings decorated the page. She tapped the tip of her pen against the name and smiled to herself. Jotting down names was a habit she'd started in high school after she'd once called a boy to talk and had become so nervous that she'd forgotten his name. She could still recall her frantic stammering.

At the time she'd been so humiliated that it had seemed only death could save her. Determined to never again repeat the mistake, she'd begun writing down the names of people she was calling.

She doubted, though, that she would ever forget the name Philip Grant.

She had dated him for three months during her sophomore year at college. She had been immediately attracted to him when they had met at a pizza parlor near campus. He was tall, but not slender like most tall men. He was beefy, strong, and incredibly rugged looking. He had been a senior, a communications major. He had seemed the type who was born for success.

As she sat with her hand on the phone, she could recall his great sense of humor and easy smile. But she could also remember why she'd stopped seeing him.

He'd had the shortest fuse of any man she'd ever met. Of course, he had never been violent with her, but during their three months together, she'd seen him become embroiled in fights and several near-fights.

The first incident had occurred when someone had accidentally jarred her in line for popcorn at a movie. Philip had faced down the offender with a look of pure predatory hunger and the nearest thing she'd ever heard to an actual human snarl.

Another time he'd pinned someone to the wall for making a rude comment about the New Orleans Saints shirt he was wearing.

Their final date had ended at a nightclub when Philip punched out someone who'd asked Rebecca to dance.

The word *fight* couldn't really be used to describe what had happened that night. Philip had been a Golden Gloves boxer in high school, and he'd simply jabbed his opponent twice in the forehead, then swung a heavy hook into his jaw, sending him in a heap to the floor.

Rebecca had been so outraged at his behavior that she'd taken a cab home. Philip had called several times, each time proclaiming his sorrow about the incident and each time asking Rebecca to give him one more chance. She hadn't.

Now she was going to call and ask for his help in locating her father.

She had never expected to see him again. It had been through only the purest stroke of luck that she'd spotted his face on the Wednesday evening newscast.

Unable to sleep and without a book to read, she'd flipped on the TV just in time to catch the end of his report. She couldn't help but feel happy for him. She knew that he had wanted to be a television journalist.

She remembered that he had planned to intern for a semester at a television station in Los Angeles and then move to Minnesota, where for some reason he was certain that he could land a job in TV news.

He must have done something right, she reasoned. From what she had seen, Philip was now part of the Channel 6 Newstrackers investigative journalism team.

After the stonewalling she had received from state adoption agencies and after unsatisfactory inquiries at private-adoption research firms, she had all but given up hope for a speedy resolution of the case.

Seeing Philip on TV, though, had given her falling spirits a much needed boost.

A siren wailing on the nearby freeway jolted her from her thoughts. It was now or never, she thought. The world wouldn't come to an end if he laughed at her and said no.

Below Philip's name on the sheet of tablet paper was the station's phone number. His personal number hadn't been listed in the directory. She punched the numbers quickly before she lost her courage.

The phone was answered by a pleasant-sounding receptionist, who wasted little time transferring the call. A short interlude of elevator music filled the line, then an electronic tone, and a man's voice answered.

"Newstrackers, Philip Grant speaking."

"Philip?" Rebecca asked. Suddenly the words she'd wanted to say were lost.

"Speaking."

She ordered herself to relax. She licked her lips and stopped worrying about her planned speech. She simply let the words flow. "Philip," she said again, "I don't know if you're going to remember me, but—"

"Rebecca?" he suddenly interrupted, his voice a question mark. "Is that you?"

She laughed lightly. "I'm surprised you remembered."

"Remembered? How could I forget?"

Rebecca was suddenly seized by the fear that Philip had confused her with someone else. Besides the fighting, which seemed to be a way of life for Philip, nothing memorable had ever occurred on their dates.

"We dated a few months when you were a senior—"

"Like I said, how could I forget?"

At least he knew who she was, though she had no idea what could have been so momentous about the time they'd shared.

Afraid that Philip might think she was simply being social, Rebecca immediately began discussing the purpose of her call. "I'm visiting from LA," she said.

"Is that right? Still living in Fullerton?"

"Pomona," she answered. His manner certainly seemed friendly enough. She filled him in briefly on her teaching job. "Anyway," she continued, trying to get back on track, "I saw you on television last night."

Philip laughed. "Yeah," he said, reminiscing aloud about the story. "Those guys were spraying insecticide all over the kitchen. It's a wonder that no one was poisoned."

"It was a good piece," Rebecca said, neglecting to mention that she'd caught only the tail end of the segment.

"And it was fun too. The second they saw me coming up the sidewalk, they knew they were in trouble." He laughed again. "I love going after the bad guys."

"Then you might be interested in a story I have for you."

"Really?" To Rebecca it sounded almost like a yawn.

She gave a short, self-conscious chuckle. "Actually, it's more of a personal favor."

"What is it?" he asked, suddenly sounding more interested.

She plunged forward. "You remember that I'm adopted?"

"Right," he answered matter-of-factly. "And your birthday is really August fifth, not the third."

Rebecca couldn't help but feel flattered that he'd remembered. "There's a chance that I might be able to locate my father," she said. "I have an idea that he's living in Phoenix."

"And you need some help tracking him down?"

She immediately felt pangs of guilt for having called. "I know that it's been a long time."

"Three years," Philip answered without hesitation.

His uncanny recall was beginning to set her on edge. "I'm sure that you probably have better things to do, but this case does have some bizarre turns that you might find interesting. And there's definitely a bad guy."

She quickly filled him in on Delbert Tipton's call and his subsequent murder.

"That's quite a story," Philip said when she had finished. "So you came to Phoenix to see if you could learn anything."

"It seems logical, doesn't it?"

"It's your only lead," he agreed. "But like you said, adoption agencies are going to be a brick wall. Tipton said that he was working against a deadline of some kind, so you really can't waste a lot of time tracking down leads that might not pan out." The line was silent for a moment. "We could always investigate Tipton and try to discover who his client was from that end."

Rebecca noted Philip's use of the word *we*. He would help her. She could almost hear him thinking over the phone. She wondered if he still pinched his upper lip between his thumb and finger when he was concentrating.

''I'll tell you what,'' he said. ''I've got some work to do until about seven o'clock. What do you say we get together on this thing at about eight? We could discuss it over dinner.''

She didn't need much time to mull it over. She hadn't had a date in over three months. Of course, McDill School wasn't exactly ideal for meeting men, and she shunned the usual pickup joints.

''Dinner sounds fine,'' she said, getting a hold of herself. This wasn't a date, after all; it was business. ''But let's keep it cheap. I'm on a pretty tight budget. A trip to Phoenix wasn't in my summer plans until yesterday.''

Philip laughed. ''Where are you staying? I'll swing by and pick you up.''

Rebecca felt a twinge of disappointment. She had half hoped that Philip would insist on paying for the meal. She smiled at her selfishness. ''I've rented a car,'' she answered. ''I could meet you.''

''I thought you were on a budget. I wouldn't want you burning up gas. Anyway, with all the roads that are torn up around this town, you'd probably get hopelessly lost within minutes.''

Rebecca grinned. ''Do you know where the Painted Sands Motel is?''

''Over by the airport, right?'' Philip paused. ''You really must be on a budget,'' he said with a laugh.

''It's not exactly the Ritz,'' Rebecca agreed.

* * *

The hours seemed to crawl by. Rebecca liked the possibility of using Tipton's records to help locate her father but had had no luck contacting his office.

She dialed Tipton's number again, and again listened as the answering machine picked up and asked her to leave a message. Strange, she thought, that his secretary wasn't in. She was beginning to doubt that he'd had one.

Not knowing who would be listening to the tape, she again hung up without leaving a message.

Frustrated, she turned on the TV and plopped onto the edge of the bed, hoping to take her mind off the case. She had called the Los Angeles police earlier in the day, but they had given her no information. With her limited budget, she wondered if it had been wise to come to Phoenix in search of her father. But even as she weighed the possibility of returning to Pomona, she knew she had no choice but to stay.

Deep down, at the very core of her soul, rumblings had begun. Yearnings she'd thought were long gone were again stirring. The need to know her true identity was once again pushing itself to the surface, and this time, she knew, she would not be able to ignore it.

Tom and Rosemary Brown, her adoptive parents, had kept an old family Bible in the maple bookcase in the family room. Inside that Bible had been several folded sheets of paper, each one documenting the Brown family history.

Rebecca remembered examining the neatly arranged branches of the family tree, too young at the time to realize that Vernon Brown, who had been born in 1873, could not have been her great-grandfather.

Searching through the family papers had given her a sense of history. She could still recall the emptiness she'd felt when it had finally dawned on her that the family whose ancestry had so interested her was not her own. Now, she knew, she wanted that ancestry. She needed it.

The television screen flickered before Rebecca's unseeing eyes.

She was certain that the Browns would have encouraged her new search, just as they had encouraged her in her first endeavor after graduating from high school. She couldn't help but wonder, though, how much of that encouragement had been thinly disguised bravery masking broken hearts.

When they had been killed on the freeway coming to pick her up at college for summer vacation at the end of her freshman year, she had vowed to never again investigate her background. She felt the search had cheapened them and their love for her. She'd finished college on the life insurance they'd left.

But she knew a void would remain in her life until she learned the identity of her natural parents. She also knew that nothing and no one could replace the love of Tom and Rosemary Brown. They were gone now, but they would live in her heart and thoughts forever.

An advertisement for a local used-car dealership suddenly blared from the set. The noisy fast talk jolted Rebecca from her solemn thoughts. She stood and turned it off.

It wouldn't do her any good, she knew, to dredge up old doubts and memories. She watched the traffic streaming along the freeway and wondered where everyone could possibly be going.

Towering palms and wide berms of bright-green grass lined the road. The sky over the city was a light, robin's-egg blue that seemed to stretch endlessly in all directions, and everywhere she looked, Rebecca caught the glint and shimmer of dancing sunlight.

The cheery view helped brighten her spirits. The past was history, and nothing could change it, but she could begin writing her future today. It was as loaded with possibility as she wanted. Moping in her motel room, though, would never make dreams come true.

She snatched her keys from atop the bureau, and then, not knowing exactly where she was going, she headed out into the afternoon for a walk.

The dry heat of the desert surrounded her as she strolled toward a mall on a nearby corner. A jet coming in for a landing thundered overhead. She wasn't planning on buying anything, but she was carrying some money just in case. The fresh air and hustle of the city enlivened her, and soon the melancholy she had been feeling was gone.

She wandered slowly through the mall, thinking of all the things she would buy if she had the money. She had always enjoyed window-shopping, but had never been able to come home completely empty-handed.

A bottle of men's fragrance on a glass shelf caught her eye. She picked it up and sniffed at the cap, thinking of Philip. NightShade. She liked it. She considered buying it for him, then almost laughed aloud at the idea. She hadn't seen him in three years.

Philip wasn't the only man Rebecca had ever turned down, but he had been one of the most persistent. He had called so many times, asking for just one more chance, that when he'd finally given up for good, Rebecca had begun feeling sorry for him, and herself, and had often wondered what might have come from one more date.

She set the bottle back on the shelf with a clink and walked out of the store.

Certainly none of the men she'd dated recently had been worth her time. She would go out of her way to make them happy, but they would do nothing for her. For three months she'd stayed at home, avoiding them. It had been a lonely time.

She had intended the walk to cheer her up, but it was beginning to have just the opposite effect. She forced the unpleasant memories from her mind and entered a pet shop. A pair of tiny black puppies frolicked in an open, glass-walled pen in the center of the floor. They were so cute together, she wondered how anyone would be able to purchase just one.

"May I help you?"

Rebecca turned and found herself face-to-face with a handsome clerk. "I was just looking," she said with a smile.

"So was I," he said.

A blush heated her cheeks, and Rebecca turned to the puppies. They were rolling and jumping over each other. "They're quite a pair."

The clerk grinned. He stepped forward and leaned against the glass pen. "Can I interest you in anything?" he asked.

"Not today," she answered with a quick smile.

"Then maybe you ought to try again tomorrow."

Rebecca laughed lightly. She had never had any trouble attracting men, but she had learned early on that the greater the scrutiny of a man's eye, the lower his intentions.

In the bright sunlight once again, she found herself smiling. Though she never allowed herself to be picked up, she was usually flattered by a man's attention. She decided that she would return to her room and begin getting ready to meet Philip.

She wound her way through the maze of cars parked in the mall's lot and crossed the street to her motel. The sun was still high in the sky, but the afternoon was drawing to a close and rush hour was beginning to snarl traffic.

As she reached the stairway that led to the second floor, someone called to her, "Excuse me!"

She stopped and a heavyset man pushed himself from the driver's seat of a beat-up Volkswagen hatchback.

Rebecca was immediately suspicious. He had been sitting in his car with the door open. He was wearing a tan corduroy sports coat. In the Arizona heat he must have been sweltering. Pulled low on his head was a tall, brown-suede cowboy hat, on the front of which was attached a large pin of the Arizona state flag. His face was shiny with sweat.

She glanced across the wide expanse of parking lot that separated her from the traffic passing on the street and tried to judge her chances of running across the man's path if she had to make a break for the lobby.

The man slid his hand under his sports coat and rubbed his large stomach. His white shirt was unbuttoned and splotched with sweat.

"Rebecca Brown?" His voice was high-pitched, almost comical for his size.

Rebecca felt a quick tug of fear. "Who are you?" she asked, easing backward slowly, ready to run if she had to.

"No use playing, honey," he said. The more he spoke, the more she noticed his southwestern cowboy drawl. "I know who you are, and I know your daddy's name."

Rebecca gasped.

The man cackled with laughter. "Now don't you be afraid," he said. "I didn't kill that guy in the hotel." He reached into his sports coat. "Take it easy, honey. I'm just going for my ID."

He withdrew a battered, black vinyl ID wallet.

"Robert James Pepper," he announced. "Private investigator."

Rebecca's pounding heart slowed slightly. "Were you working with Tipton?" she asked.

"Not exactly."

She eyed him intently. He flashed her a mocking grin that displayed rows of crooked, tobacco-stained teeth.

She shuddered. "If you aren't Tipton's partner, who are you?"

He cackled again and handed her the identification. "We were working on the same case, but for different reasons, you might say."

Rebecca scanned the ID card. It carried official-looking seals and endorsements, but she had no way of knowing if it was genuine. "What do you mean, different reasons?"

"Well, honey," he said, "it seems some people want you found, and others don't."

Rebecca remained silent. A steady stream of traffic noises rolled across the parking lot. If he tried anything funny, she'd make a break for the road. Judging by his figure, he would be easy to outrun.

"I just want a little information," Pepper said.

She faced him silently. She was becoming aware of the heat, standing as she was in the parking lot, unprotected from the sun.

"I just want to know what Tipton told you," he said.

He faced her for several seconds while she tried to decide if she should answer. Suddenly a question occurred to her. "How did you know that I knew Tipton?"

His hand slid under his shirt and rubbed his chest. "I wouldn't have if you hadn't shown up at his hotel. I was just following him, see, wondering where he would take me. Then you showed up."

"Then," Rebecca was quick to point out, "you must have seen who killed him."

Pepper cackled long and loud. "Well, now, honey, you see, that's where it gets a little embarrassing. I'd been on his tail all day long and, well. . . ." He patted his stomach. "A man's got to eat, you know."

Rebecca narrowed her eyes in suspicion; a thin shiver ran up her spine. She might be talking with a murderer.

"You were gone when he was killed?" she asked, coloring the question with doubt.

"It's hard to swallow, ain't it?" He shook his head to prove that he couldn't believe it himself. "I wasn't gone but an hour, and when I came back. . . . Well, you were there, along with about a whole army of cops."

"You've been following me since then?" she asked. The thought raised gooseflesh over her entire body.

"Don't let it scare you," he said, his manner anything but reassuring. "I've got a job to do. Just like anyone else, you know. So just tell me what Tipton had to say, and I'll be on my way."

"I'm not going to tell you anything."

Pepper shrugged, pretending he couldn't have cared less. "Have it your way," he said. "But I'm here to tell you that if you think you're going to find your father without my help, you're thinking wrong."

Rebecca gambled. "I've been in touch with Tipton's secretary," she lied. "I already know who my father is."

Pepper erupted in laughter, and Rebecca was immediately sorry that she'd said anything.

"His secretary?" he asked when he'd finally gained control of himself. "His secretary?" he asked again. "Honey, I know for a fact that Delbert Tipton worked out of his tiny little silver mobile home in a crummy lot on the south side of Tucson. I don't think he had enough room in there for a typewriter, much less a secretary." He laughed again and let it die off slowly into his high-pitched cackle.

"Well," he said at last, adjusting his hat on his head. "I guess if you've been talking to his secretary, you must just about know it all.'' He paused for a moment to rub his stomach. '' 'Course, if there's anything you think you might be lacking in, you might want to give me a call.'' He reached into the pocket of his sports coat and handed her his card.

Rebecca snatched it from him.

''I figured you'd want that,'' he said. ''Now that's my own personal number. Don't you go giving it out. I'll be getting phone calls from every pretty young thing between here and Albuquerque.''

''I don't think you have to worry about that,'' Rebecca said dryly, trying to reclaim some of her injured pride. Pepper had just made a fool of her.

He broke into another phony grin. ''I suppose you're right,'' he said, rubbing his stomach. ''Good-bye.''

Rebecca watched him cross the parking lot and climb into his faded green car. He waited for a break in traffic, then pulled into the street and was lost in the rush-hour crunch.

She waited several minutes before returning to her room. She realized with a shudder how easy it had been for him to follow her. She had never suspected a thing.

That would change, she thought to herself as she climbed the stairs to her room.

Chapter Four

Philip listened attentively as Rebecca filled him in on her meeting with Pepper, interrupting her occasionally to clarify a point.

They were seated at a corner table of Little Lucky's, a modest-sized Italian restaurant near downtown. A stub of candle flickered in the empty Chianti bottle that served as a holder. The two blended well with the fashionably casual clientele.

"You're going to have to find a new room," he told her when she had finished. "I've dealt with private investigators before. Most of them are honest, but occasionally you run across one who's more interested in uncovering money than uncovering facts. This one's been following you for a few days, and that doesn't sound good."

"My first thought was that he'd killed Tipton," Rebecca said.

"Anything's possible," Philip commented, "but I doubt that he had anything to do with it, or else he wouldn't have shown himself to you today."

Rebecca nodded. She had called the Los Angeles police to report Pepper's sudden appearance and his connection with the case. She had received an assurance that the Phoenix police would be notified.

"Frankly," she said, "both those private investigators gave me the creeps."

Philip laughed. "They're definitely a different breed," he said. He sipped from a glass of ice water. "What interests me is Pepper's comment about some people wanting you found and others not wanting that to happen."

Rebecca agreed. She had been mulling it over for hours. "I know what it's like to be an orphan," she began. "And I suppose that helps me understand why my father should suddenly begin searching for me."

She rubbed her finger absently along the knife at her place setting. "You want to know," she said. "You want to know something, anything." She smiled at Philip. "I know we've talked about this before. But no matter how much we discuss it, you can't possibly feel what it's like to not know who your parents are, to not know something as basic as what they look like."

Philip was silent for a moment before answering. "I may not feel what you feel," he said, "but I can understand." He reached across the table and patted her hands gently.

For a moment their eyes met. A spark raced through Rebecca. His hands were warm and caring. He was still as incredibly handsome as she'd remembered him. Of course, three years had passed. His blond hair was slightly longer now, and his shoulders seemed broader, as if he'd been pumping iron. His eyes were the same unforgettable sparkling blue. If not for his quick temper, she thought, he would be perfect.

"My father must want to know about me," she said.

"He must want to see me. But if he's married, especially to someone other than my mother, finding me could create a considerable strain."

Philip nodded thoughtfully. "So you think someone close to your father might have hired Pepper to make sure that you were never reunited."

She nodded. "What other reason could there be?"

A waiter appeared and took their order. The candle on the table flickered as he turned and left.

Philip pinched his upper lip between his thumb and forefinger. "Then, if we're putting things together correctly, it must have been Tipton who was working for your father." He paused and nodded. "But we can't say for sure who Pepper is working for."

"All we know is that he was following Tipton," Rebecca said.

Philip nodded. "Hoping to be led to you." He glanced at her. "It worked. Of course, we can't be sure of anything here. I'm inclined to agree that Tipton and Pepper were working different sides of the fence, but we can't be absolutely certain of that fact. We should consider the possibility that the two were teamed up on this in some way and that their plans went awry when Tipton was murdered."

Rebecca sighed and shook her head. "It's so confusing. Is there anything we can do on our own that might shed some light on my father's identity?"

Philip shrugged. "You know better than I how difficult it is to cut through the layers of red tape surrounding adoption cases."

The hope she had been holding out for Philip's expertise began to wither. She had believed that with his background as an investigative reporter, he might have some ideas about how to begin the search for her father, but the tone of his voice telegraphed his feelings.

"You told me that you'd already done some checking with Arizona state adoption agencies," Philip said.

"I thought that if I'd been adopted by someone living in Arizona, they might have a record. Some of the private firms said they might be able to help, but the cost isn't cheap, and the search could take months, even years."

He looked grim. "You told me once that you knew you were born in Las Vegas. You investigated that avenue years ago, didn't you?"

Again she was amazed at his memory. "I haven't tried recently. I wouldn't expect any more success there than I've had here."

"Me, either," he agreed.

"You'd mentioned that we might be able to work backward through Tipton's files," she said.

"I was hoping we wouldn't get to this part," Philip said with a wry smile. "I tried calling his number several times this afternoon. Usually I connected with an answering machine. The last time, though, someone picked it up. The guy on the other end was pretty cagey until I identified myself as a reporter for Channel 6. That's when I discovered he was with the Pinal County sheriff's office. They'd come in to seal everything up for the LAPD. They didn't give out much information, but from what I could make out, Tipton didn't have much of a filing system. I guess he kept everything in his head. I don't think we can expect much help from that direction."

Rebecca shook her head reproachfully. "I honestly pictured him in a big office with a bunch of operatives running around. He made it sound like a professional organization. He even said I had a case number."

Philip laughed. "Remember, don't believe everything you see, and only half of what you hear." He helped himself to the last breadstick in the basket the busboy had set before them minutes earlier.

"Half might be too much," Rebecca said. She watched him munching contentedly on the breadstick. "Did you ever stop to think that I might have wanted that?" she asked.

"No." He continued chewing, then held up the uneaten portion. "Want the rest?" he asked.

"What if I said yes?"

"I didn't say I'd give it to you." He took another bite and chewed around a smug smile. Suddenly he said, "I don't know why I didn't think of it before." His eyes were alight. "I made some friends when I was interning at KXNT in Los Angeles. I might be able to get one of them to pump some information from the LAPD, just in case there's something our friend in the Pinal County sheriff's office didn't want to share."

Rebecca nodded.

"Of course," he said, "it's just an offer. I realize that you like to turn those down."

He was smiling, but she detected some hurt below the surface. "What's that supposed to mean?" she asked.

"Exactly what you think," he replied evenly. "A few years ago, when I was calling you, you wouldn't have anything to do with me. Now you want a favor, and here we are eating dinner.''

Rebecca felt herself edging toward the defensive. ''You may recall,'' she said, ''that there was a reason why I stopped seeing you.''

The waiter arrived with their food, and the conversation ceased abruptly. He set a colorful pasta salad before Rebecca and a plate of lasagna before Philip. Rebecca tried to behave casually, but Philip's comment had angered her.

''Will that be all?'' the waiter asked, sounding anxious to leave. The sudden, strained silence that had settled over the table upon his arrival seemed to make him self-conscious and awkward. ''I'm sorry the order took so long,'' he said. ''But one of the cooks is sick tonight, and—''

Rebecca realized that the waiter thought they had been talking about him.

''That's fine,'' Philip said. ''We're in no hurry.''

''Let me just get this,'' the waiter said, reaching for the empty breadstick basket. He bumped Rebecca's water glass, and it toppled over, sending a stream of ice water across the table and into her lap.

She brushed it away quickly with her napkin, only faintly hearing the waiter's repeated apologies. It was her new summer dress, her one extravagance for the summer. Then she glanced up at Philip.

Fortunately he wasn't squeezing the waiter's throat. He was, instead, leaning forward, using his napkin to wipe up the puddle atop the table.

The waiter hurriedly excused himself to find a towel.

"It's only water," Rebecca said, dabbing at her clothes.

Philip continued mopping up the table. "I doubt if you're going to want to get up and walk out anytime soon," he said.

Rebecca laughed self-consciously. "Thank goodness we have an entire dinner to wait through." Noticing the curious stares of other patrons, she added, "We're certainly getting a lot of attention."

Philip returned to his seat.

"That was a little embarrassing," she finally said, setting her soggy napkin on the table.

He smiled at her. "That's what you get for turning me down."

She grinned. "As I was saying before we were so rudely interrupted, you may recall that there was a reason for that."

"My fighting days are a thing of the past."

"Thank goodness for small favors," she said. "I was half expecting to see you knock the waiter over the table."

At that moment the waiter reappeared. He looked quickly toward Philip. "It was an accident," he said in his own defense, as if expecting Philip to leap out of his seat at him.

He dabbed quickly at the table, moving Rebecca's plate and utensils to the side to wipe underneath them. He glanced nervously back to Philip, explaining in short, quick sentences just how sorry he was. He apologized again to Rebecca and quickly disappeared.

"Anyway," Philip continued, "I learned my lesson about fighting long ago."

"Oh, really?" Rebecca asked, not sure if she could believe him. "And what led to this revelation?"

"In the first place, I met a guy at a gas pump who knew karate."

She laughed. "And in the second place?"

"In the second place," he said. "In the second place, I lost a chance at you. So I got some counseling on learning how to handle my temper and deal with problems in a more mature way."

Rebecca was silent, stunned and slightly embarrassed by the frank admission. She'd had no idea that she'd meant so much to him.

"I know that you'll only be here for a few days," he said, "but let's have some fun together."

"How can you be sure that I'm not seeing someone who might get jealous?" she asked.

"Are you?"

She laughed. "No."

"What does that mean? Are you not seeing anyone, or are you not seeing anyone who might get jealous?" He shook his head as if to clear his thoughts.

She laughed again. "It doesn't matter. The answer is no."

He smiled. "For once it's good to hear you say that."

They lapsed into conversation about past times. The more they talked, the more Rebecca remembered the happy times they had spent together.

"How did you happen to end up in Phoenix?" she asked. "I thought you were heading for Minnesota."

"Have you ever spent a winter in St. Paul? I'm a

southern California boy. Cold is something I don't enjoy.''

''I always wondered why you were so intent on getting a job up there,'' she said.

He shrugged. ''I try to live as independently as possible. On those rare occasions when I'm not quite so independent, I at least like people to think I am. There aren't many people who know the truth about that job.''

''What is the truth?''

He grinned sheepishly. ''My uncle owned the station,'' he said.

Rebecca laughed. ''I'm glad to hear that nepotism is alive and well.''

''It gave me a break. I got into a story about illegal dumping up there and really earned my wings. When Channel 6 made an offer, I jumped at it.''

''So here you are in Phoenix, working as an investigative reporter for Channel 6.''

He nodded. ''To tell you the truth, I'm not sure I like investigative journalism. I never see the bright side of anything. Sometimes I think everyone in Arizona is on the take.'' He smiled at her. ''Of course, what's bad for people is good for me. With all the scandals that are constantly cropping up, my job is practically guaranteed.''

''You're beginning to sound a little cynical.''

''The fortunes of war. However, I may be able to put all the corruption and raw deals behind me. I have an opportunity for an extended assignment in Antarctica. Researchers at the University of Arizona have devised a scheme for measuring past changes in the composition of the Earth's atmosphere through the spectroscopic analysis of deep ice cores.

"The job is something of a plum, really," he continued. "Six months on the ice might not sound too appealing, but we'll get a good documentary out of it. This study could revolutionize our understanding of the Earth's formation. I could really make a name for myself."

"It sounds exciting," Rebecca said, feigning enthusiasm. They had been reunited just in time to be parted once again. "How soon would you be leaving?"

"The funding's already in. The project is set. I'm just waiting for the word. Confidentially, I've already been told that the job is mine. All I need is official confirmation."

She listened with sinking spirits. In the back of her mind she had been hoping for a reunion. But Philip, she realized, had his own life now. She had been expecting too much to actually believe that romance could have blossomed after so much time. If only, three years earlier, she'd accepted one last offer for a date, things might have been so very different.

Philip took the check when it arrived. "How much do I owe?" she asked, opening her wallet.

He looked absolutely astounded. "You must be joking!"

"No, I want to pay. This isn't a date, after all. You weren't planning on seeing me tonight."

"Put that away," he said quietly, nodding toward her wallet and sounding offended. "I'm paying."

She dropped the wallet back into her purse. "Only if it will make you happy," she said with a smile.

"Happy doesn't exactly describe it." He paid the check and they left.

"The first thing we have to do," he said as they crossed the parking lot, "is find a new place for you to stay. I don't like the idea of these private investigators sneaking up on you."

An older couple, on their way into the restaurant, passed them.

"You could always stay at my place," he offered, and Rebecca noted the hopeful tone in his voice, which he tried to disguise with a laugh.

Before she could answer, a high-pitched voice called to them from across the lot.

"I wouldn't be in such a hurry to leave, Miss Brown."

The two turned toward the voice. A heavy man in a cowboy hat leaned against the side of a battered, faded, Volkswagen hatchback.

"Don't tell me," Philip said. "Let me guess. Robert Pepper."

Chapter Five

"Well, this sure is cozy," Pepper said, eyeing the pair as they approached him. "Didn't take you long to find a reporter to talk to, did it?"

Rebecca felt fear from her vulnerability mixing with anger. How dare he continue to follow her! "We're friends," she told him.

"I'll just bet you are," he said; then he turned to Philip. "I know I've seen you on TV, but I can't remember your name."

Philip introduced himself.

"Nope, never heard of you before," Pepper said, cackling at his own joke. "I'll bet you're interested in this story."

"I've been filled in."

"I'll just bet you have," Pepper scoffed. "Now I'm going to fill you in. My business is strictly with the little lady. I'm not saying anything to you."

"He's not here to cover the story," Rebecca said.

"Of course not," Pepper sneered. "He just popped right up out of nowhere, like one of those jack-in-the-box clowns." He eyed Philip closely. "A fifty-cent clown with a fifty-dollar haircut."

"She said we were friends," Philip repeated, his voice hard and flat. "She wasn't lying. Now if you've got something to say, say it. We don't have all night to stand here and listen to you drool."

Pepper stepped away from the car, tugging up the waistband of his pants. He still wore the corduroy jacket. He approached Philip. "I don't drool, chief, and I don't stutter. I said I'm not talking to you."

Philip slipped his hand around Rebecca's arm. "We're leaving," he said. Then he turned to Pepper. "I've got a feeling that this thing is pretty important to you. I wonder what it's going to be worth after I put it on the air and blow the whole thing wide open. This is the kind of story people swarm to. I'll put it on at six o'clock, and by seven Rebecca will be talking to her father, and you, cowboy, will be standing on the street corner holding your hat, waiting for a donation."

"I expect you could be right, Mr. Grant. I certainly do expect so, except for one thing." Pepper cackled. "The old man's dead."

Philip stopped short. Rebecca pulled herself free from his grip and turned to face Pepper. "Dead?" she asked, unbelieving.

"Guess you don't know as much as you thought you did, newshound. But I'll tell you what," he said to Rebecca, affecting a syrupy tone. "If you want to talk to the old bird, I might be able to arrange something with the phone company—you know, extra-long distance." He cackled again.

Rebecca felt as though she'd been punched in the stomach. She seemed unable to catch her breath, and her mouth was suddenly dry.

"It's all right," she heard Philip saying. A comforting hand stroked her shoulders.

"Looks like you just saw a scary movie, honey," Pepper said.

"You'd better shut up, Tex."

"One of them monster movies."

Rebecca barely heard. Dead. Her father. She hadn't realized how badly she'd wanted to meet him until this instant. She was filled with an empty, tearless sorrow.

"Relax," Philip was saying.

She noticed how ragged her breathing sounded and forced control on herself. It was so unfair. She had never stopped wondering who her natural parents were, and now, just when she had thought she was so close to meeting her father, to learn that he was dead. . . .

She tried to regain her composure.

"It's all right," Philip said. "I'm here." He wrapped his arm soothingly around her shoulders, holding her, giving her comfort.

Rebecca breathed deeply and closed her eyes. "I'm fine," she said at last. She reached up and laid her hand over Philip's on her shoulder. "It took me by surprise, that's all."

"I thought it would," Pepper said.

Philip's tone was calm, but his tone was menacing. "You'd better back off."

"I wish I could," Pepper responded. "I really wish I could. But I can't, you see. We're running out of time."

"We're going to have to make the time," Philip said.

Pepper turned his attention to Rebecca. "It seems to me that you're taking the news a little too hard," he said.

"Considering that you never met the old bird and that he gave you away when you were just a teeny-tiny, helpless little baby."

"That's it." Philip stepped from Rebecca, his hands clenched into fists.

"Stop, Philip!" she called. She couldn't bear to see a fight now.

"Yeah, stop, Philip," Pepper echoed, hitching a thumb under his belt and sliding his hand along his waistband, pushing open the front of the sports coat and exposing a pistol in a shoulder holster.

Philip stood frozen between the two, his fists raised, knowing there would be no fight. Finally he dropped his hands, flexed his fingers, and returned to Rebecca's side.

"That's using the old bean," Pepper said, letting the jacket fall closed. "Now, the old man's dead, and there's nothing we can do about that. But he left a will, and there is something we can do about that."

Philip slid his arm around Rebecca's shoulders and pulled her tightly to him. "So you're trying to settle a will," he said.

"That got your ears perked, did it?"

"We're listening."

"Not here, you're not," Pepper countered. "I'm not going to wait here for some camera to get popped into my face."

"I told you I'm not covering the story."

"You also told me you were going to put it on at six o'clock. What am I supposed to believe?"

Philip's hand rubbed gently along Rebecca's arm. Pepper had them, she knew. He was going to call the shots.

"Where?" Philip asked at last.

"Let's take a ride," Pepper said.

"My car's over there." Philip jerked his head vaguely across the lot.

"I know where it is. But I'm not getting in a car with you at the wheel. No telling where it might end up. Maybe even on the wrong end of a camera." Pepper gestured toward his own car.

Rebecca refused to climb into this repulsive man's car. "We'll take a cab," she said.

The trio returned to the restaurant, where Philip called a cab.

"Take us down Central," Pepper ordered as he climbed into the backseat. Philip took the middle, and Rebecca sat against the other door.

Pepper waited until the cab had merged with traffic before he began talking. He spoke in low tones.

"Your father died more than six months ago," he said. "It wasn't until they read the will that anyone even knew he had a daughter. He was never married, see, so everyone was surprised to learn that he had a kid."

Rebecca listened quietly. She watched traffic rushing past Pepper's window. Headlights threw long shadows throughout the car.

"Tipton was hired by the estate to find you. But, like I said, some people don't want that to happen." He reached into his sports coat and withdrew a pack of cigarettes and a large silver lighter.

"You saw what happened to Tipton," he said, lighting up. "That's the risk of doing business." He flipped the lighter closed. "I guess you already figured it out that I'm working for someone who doesn't want you found."

A shiver of fear raced down Rebecca's spine. "Then you must know who killed Tipton."

Pepper laughed as though she had made a joke. "My client doesn't have the guts for killing," he said. "But he does want to make a deal." He leaned forward and peered over the driver's shoulder into the rearview mirror.

"Something wrong?" Philip asked.

Pepper chuckled. "I wasn't looking for spinach in my teeth."

Philip turned and surveyed the road behind him. Spotting nothing suspicious, he again faced the front.

"You were talking about a deal," he prompted.

"You don't forget much, do you?" Tipton said. He faced Rebecca. "My client wants to deal with you"—he jerked his lit cigarette at Philip—"not him." He glanced forward into the mirror once more. "Let's get one thing straight right from the start. I'm going to call my client 'he,' but that doesn't necessarily mean it's a man. It's just the way I talk." He glanced once more at Philip. "I guess I'm just an old-fashioned cowboy," he said and cackled. "Anyway," he went on, picking a speck of tobacco from his tongue, "my client doesn't want the long-lost daughter to return. He's afraid of . . . complications."

"Why should he be afraid of me?" Rebecca asked. "I only want to know my father's identity."

"That's all you want today. Next week your story might change."

"What are you getting at?" Philip asked.

Pepper took a long drag from his cigarette and let the smoke slowly trickle into Philip's face. "Now there's a real reporter for you," he said, speaking to Rebecca. "Always digging for the facts."

He smiled at her, displaying his hideous teeth, and did his best impersonation of a concerned father. "Honey," he said, "if it was up to me, I'd just give you the name of your daddy and let it go at that. If it was up to me, that's exactly what I'd do. But it isn't up to me, you see? I'm working for someone else now, so I can't just give anything away to you."

"Spare me the sympathy," Rebecca snapped. "You're not in this out of any sense of civic spirit; you're in this for yourself. Now, what kind of deal do you want to make?"

Pepper cackled. "You've been around this fellow for too long, honey." He glanced at Philip. "He's going to pollute your mind. You've got to learn how to listen."

He leaned forward, checked the rearview mirror, and ordered the driver to take the next right.

"Are we being followed?" Philip asked.

"Are we?"

"We're not in this cab for our health," Philip said. "We didn't come along to listen to your pearls of wisdom. You wanted to talk business, so talk."

"Okay, okay," Pepper said, inhaling again on the cigarette. By now the wafting smoke was beginning to burn Rebecca's eyes. He faced her. "I'm going to give you fifty thousand dollars to give up the search," he said.

Rebecca was astounded. What could possibly be so important that it was worth fifty thousand dollars?

Pepper grinned lazily. "That didn't catch you napping, did it?" he asked. He glanced at the back of the driver's head. "Make the next right," he said.

"Why would anyone want to buy me off for fifty thousand dollars?" Rebecca asked.

"It's got to be worth more," Philip said. "Much more."

"That's right," Pepper confirmed. "Listen to the cub reporter here. He probably knows more about this than me." He ordered the driver to make another right.

"Someone must be playing for high stakes to offer an amount like that," Philip told Rebecca. "I'd turn it down until we have a chance to think this through."

"You don't get another chance," Pepper said, withdrawing a long folded paper from inside his sports coat. "I took the liberty of bringing a contract along. You can sign now, Miss Brown, or never." He unfolded the document and handed it to her. Philip intercepted it.

"I won't sign it," Rebecca insisted.

Philip nodded encouragement, quickly scanning the document. "This contract would require you never again to initiate a search for your father," he said. "You might be signing away a fortune."

"This isn't about money, Philip." Her voice held a bite. "This has to do with finding out who I am and where I come from." She stared pointedly through the front windshield. "I thought you understood."

Philip was silent as he folded the contract. "I'm sorry," he said quietly, handing the paper back to Pepper.

"You're making a mistake," Pepper warned. "You'll never find him. You don't stand a chance."

Rebecca's hope was quickly draining away. Pepper was probably right, she knew. If people were working to keep her father's identity a secret, it would remain a secret.

"We'll find him," Philip promised.

Pepper snorted. He ordered the driver to return to Little Lucky's. "We're all going home empty tonight," he said, turning to glance through the rear window. "The little lady's going home empty, I'm going home empty, and you," he said, speaking to Philip, "you're going home empty too. You and that camera crew you've had following us."

"What are you talking about?" Philip asked, agitated and angry.

"I'll just bet you don't know," Pepper answered facetiously. "The white sedan that's been following us since we left the restaurant."

Both Rebecca and Philip turned to look out the window.

"Can't see it now," Pepper continued. "But it's back there. Pretty clumsy job of tailing. You ought to speak to the driver. They followed us right through a whole string of right turns." He snorted. "Amateurs."

"We don't have a camera crew on our tail," Philip said. "Do you think they have nothing better to do than sit in a parking lot waiting for you to show up?"

"I didn't say they were waiting," Pepper answered. "I expect you called them at the same time you dialed the cab. Would have been a heck of a scoop, helping this poor little thing find her father. 'Course, doesn't make any difference. Putting it on the tube isn't going to help you one little bit."

"I didn't call anyone but a cab," Philip said.

Pepper shrugged. "Doesn't matter." He tapped the contract in his sports coat pocket. "You'd better think this over."

"I don't need to," Rebecca answered.

The trip continued in silence until the cab pulled to a stop in front of Little Lucky's. Pepper reached into his wallet and pulled out a bill. "That's my share of the fare," he told Philip. "Hope you don't mind that I divided it by three."

Philip tossed the bill back at him. "Keep it," he said. "My treat."

"I get expenses," Pepper insisted. He crumpled the bill and flipped it onto Philip's lap. "Don't spend it all in one place." He leaned against the door and slammed it shut with his hip. Then, suddenly, he turned and opened it. "In case you change your mind," he said, "you can call me tomorrow. 'Course, you won't get fifty grand for it. That was a one-time-only offer. The payoff drops with every hour."

He looked about ready to slam the door when he added, "One more thing I almost forgot. Time is running out. According to the will, you only have until tomorrow midnight to be found. After that, it won't matter, anyway." He winked at Rebecca, then finally slammed the door closed.

Philip paid off and tipped the cabbie; then he and Rebecca returned to his car. Pepper was just driving off the lot.

''You're staying with me tonight,'' Philip said.

Rebecca appraised him coldly. ''I can manage by myself,'' she told him. ''Just drive me back to my motel.''

Philip laid a hand on her shoulder. ''What is it? What's the matter?''

''You're the matter,'' she said, shrugging his arm away. ''I can't believe how you were behaving in that cab with Pepper, trying to figure the angles and looking for a big payoff.''

Philip tucked his hands into his pockets. ''I'm sorry,'' he said. ''I guess I got a little carried away.''

''I guess so,'' she retorted. She attempted to keep the anger in her voice, but she could already feel it running down. Philip, she knew, had only been acting in what he'd believed were her best interests. Still, she couldn't keep herself from landing one last barb. ''We're not on a treasure hunt.''

Philip's eyes suddenly hardened. ''Maybe not, but there's money involved. And you can bet that it's big money. My guess is that you're set up for a large inheritance. Tipton was killed because he was going to lead you to it. You heard Pepper; you have until midnight tomorrow to show yourself.'' He eyed her significantly. ''Pepper let out an awful lot of information. Obviously, others are named in the will. I'm betting that if you show up, they'll be forced to take a substantial cut in their share.''

Suddenly Rebecca was scared. ''Do you think someone might try to prevent me from claiming my inheritance?''

Philip avoided answering her question directly. ''You've seen how easy it was for Pepper to follow you.''

Rebecca glanced involuntarily over her shoulder. ''Anyone could be following me.'' Then she had a chilling thought. ''The white sedan.''

Philip slowly scanned the area around the parking lot. ''I know it wasn't a camera crew,'' he said. He opened her door. ''Get in. We're going for a ride.''

''Where to?'' she asked.

''We'll know when we get there,'' he said, turning the key. The engine revved to life, and they pulled into the busy traffic on the street.

Chapter Six

The first hint of morning light dribbled through a crack in the curtains, painting a thin, gray stroke on the wall of her room. Rebecca had slept fitfully and was relieved to see that the long night was finally coming to an end.

She kicked off her sheets and climbed from bed. They hadn't returned to the Painted Sands Motel after leaving the restaurant, but had found a new place to stay after driving for an hour through the city along a twisting, winding, serpentine maze of roads. Satisfied that they could not have been followed, they had taken the freeway north and had finally pulled in at a motel just beyond the Phoenix city limits.

Rebecca closed the door that connected her room to Philip's and switched on the light. The long drive and constant fear of being followed had wreaked havoc on her nerves. By the time she and Philip had registered, she had convinced herself that every car passing on the freeway carried a killer and that a murderer lurked in every shadow. Philip had agreed to keep the door between their rooms open, "just in case."

She faced herself in the bathroom mirror and couldn't help but smile at the disheveled, haggard face that returned her stare. Somehow the break of day focused all her worries of the night before into a single, ridiculous joke. She had allowed her imagination to run away with her. She had even slept in her clothes, in case she had needed to make a fast escape.

She ran her fingers through the tangle of her hair. Her shampoo, makeup, and fresh clothes were back at the Painted Sands. Here she had only a tiny bar of soap and a towel. Taking one last look at her bleary eyes, she decided that it was better than nothing.

She began running the shower but turned it off. Philip was still sleeping and, ridiculous as it seemed, she was scared of an undetected intruder sneaking up on her while she washed her hair. Horror movies had given her a healthy respect for her vulnerability in the shower.

She wandered back to her bed and considered trying for a little more sleep, but knew it would be impossible. She was keyed-up and anxious to solve the mystery concerning the identity of her father. She felt as if her mind were traveling in a thousand different directions. She had already been cooped up in the room for one evening. She didn't feel that she could take another minute.

She slipped out of bed, tiptoed across the floor, and silently eased open the connecting door. Philip needed his sleep, she knew. He had been just as tired as she when they had pulled in last night. She knew that he would be angry if she simply woke him up, but she couldn't stand to waste any more time in this motel room. Barely more than eighteen hours remained before the midnight deadline. She decided she would wake him, but she would do it accidentally . . . on purpose.

She turned on the TV in her room and cranked up the volume. An early-morning newscast flooded the room with sound. She stood to the side for a few seconds while the morning cotton report boomed out weevil-infestation news, then bounded over to the wide-open connecting door and slammed it shut.

Seconds later knocking sounded from Philip's room.

Rebecca opened the door a crack. "Philip?" she asked innocently.

"Were you trying to wake me up?" his voice answered, still husky with sleep.

She swung the door wide. "I'm sorry about the TV," she responded. "I closed the door so you wouldn't hear it."

"Is that right?" His hair was flattened on one side and poking straight up on the other. He had removed his shirt for sleeping and was dressed only in the slacks he'd worn to the restaurant the previous evening. "About five minutes ago I was lying there, wondering if you were awake, when I saw you close that door ever so quietly; then I heard water running for a few seconds. Next, the door opened again, very quietly. For a second there, I thought you were trying to be considerate. That's when the TV came on, and you slammed the door so hard I thought it would fly off the hinges." He flashed a quick grin at her. "If you'd wanted me to wake up, all you had to do was call to me."

Rebecca felt her cheeks redden with embarrassment. "I can't believe you were in there awake the whole time without telling me," she countered. "Anyway," she continued, feeling sheepish, "I wanted to take a shower."

"Me too," Philip said.

"Feel free," she told him. "Just as soon as I finish mine. I want you to guard me."

He laughed out loud. "You're afraid to take a shower alone?"

She attempted to hide her embarrassment under a facade of self-righteous anger. "If you had any compassion at all, you wouldn't be laughing at me. You would try to understand." She paused to be sure that her speech was having the desired effect. "After all, it wasn't you who found Tipton." The memory of Tipton's body lying face up in the tub sent a spasm of fear through her body.

"All right, all right," Philip said. "You've made your point. I'll just sit here and wait." He glanced at the TV. "Good," he said with mock enthusiasm. "The morning farm news. My favorite part of the day. I hope I haven't missed the pork-belly report." He plopped down on the side of the bed, his back to Rebecca.

"I'll see you in a few minutes," she said, putting a smile in her voice.

"Take your time. I'm not going anywhere."

Traffic was moving easily along the freeway as Rebecca and Philip made their way back into the city. After a quick breakfast they had decided to return to the Painted Sands and retrieve Rebecca's belongings.

"You can stay at my place until this thing is cleared up," he told her. "I know you don't have the money to continue living in motels, and I know you'd be safer with me around."

Rebecca smiled to herself. Safe was the last thing she

felt when she was with Philip. She had strong doubts about the wisdom of spending so much time so near to him. Already he was working himself into her life, and she was feeling a growing attraction to him. She wondered if, sharing his home, she would have the strength to resist that attraction, and she wondered if she wanted to.

"We still don't have a clue as to the identity of my father," she said, letting the thought go. She leaned forward and switched on the radio.

"I think we have more than you're willing to believe," Philip corrected. "We can make some informed guesses, at least. First, we may as well assume that your father lived in Phoenix, or somewhere nearby. Tipton was headed here, and Pepper has his office here as well."

"That's true," she agreed. "I know that we have more information now than we did yesterday, but will that be enough?"

He shrugged. "I did a story once on funeral-parlor rip-offs, when I was working in St. Paul. I learned a lot about wills and probate. It may take a while, but I think that we'll be able to make do with what we have." He glanced at Rebecca. "We know, for instance, or at least suspect, that the will entails a good deal of money. To me that means your father could have been a successful businessman or was somehow well-known in the community."

An eighteen-wheeler pulled up alongside them, its diesel engine drowning out the low tones of the radio.

"We could look through old obituaries," he continued, rolling his window closed against the truck. "In the local paper, at least, business leaders and other officials are normally listed in separate columns on the obituary page.''

Rebecca tried to conceal her doubt. ''It's a chance,'' she said.

''Remember, too, that Pepper continually referred to your father as being old. It would speed things up if we concentrated our search on men who were seventy years or older when they died.''

''But even if we did search the obituaries,'' Rebecca interjected, ''we would simply end up with a list of names. We would have no way of knowing if any of them were my father.''

Philip continued to ease the car forward, tight on the bumper of the car in front of them. ''When a person dies, the executor of the estate is required to file a form with the courts, stating his intention to act as personal representative. We simply use the list of names we take from the obituaries, then search court records to find out who the executors were for each estate.''

She nodded. ''Then we could contact the executor, to see if a search was being conducted for a missing heir.''

He smiled at her. ''Exactly.''

She chewed on her bottom lip. She doubted that the plan would work. If nothing else, it would require too much time, and they only had until midnight.

''We're counting on the fact that his obituary would be separate from the bulk of obituaries,'' she noted. ''If that isn't the case, then we won't have a chance.''

''True,'' Philip said. ''And it's an awful lot of work.'' He glanced over his shoulder and quickly changed lanes.

Rebecca felt a growing sense of hopelessness. So much had happened in the last two days. It seemed impossible that it would work itself out.

For so long, it seemed, she had lived a life of daily routine. She woke up in the morning, worked all day, then went to bed at night. Suddenly, in the course of forty-eight hours, she had been plunged from her secure world into a shadowy landscape of private investigators and murderers.

A father she had never known and with whom she had ceased to concern herself was now paramount in her life, and Philip Grant, a man she had vowed never to see again, was once again at her side.

"I thought that you had stopped chewing your nails," Philip said, interrupting her thoughts.

She pulled her finger from her mouth. "I quit daily."

"Cut them off, and you won't have to worry about it anymore."

"I think I'd prefer to chew them off slowly," she answered.

They drove several minutes longer. "I just realized," she said suddenly. "Even though our deadline is midnight tonight, we'll only have access to legal records for as long as the courts remain open."

"I'd thought of that," Philip said. "But I didn't want to mention it. In the face of everything else we have to overcome, I was afraid that it would crush your spirits."

"It doesn't help much," she agreed with a weak smile.

"There's one more thing," Philip said. She could tell by his pause that he didn't want to give voice to his thoughts. "I won't be able to help you. I've got to work."

Rebecca felt the bottom dropping out from her plans. "But there's so much work."

"Believe me, I would help you if I could. But I've been working on a project about the legislature that's going to hit the air on Friday, and there's a new scandal brewing over a land swap out on the Gila Reservation. I can't afford to miss it."

She nodded. "You couldn't have known that I was going to suddenly show up from out of nowhere," she said tightly.

"I really wish I could," he said, noting her tone.

"I can do it alone." Her eyes locked on the road ahead. She knew that the anger she was feeling was petty. Her arrival had been sudden, and Philip could hardly be blamed for having his own life. But with all that had happened—Tipton's murder and Pepper's offer of fifty thousand dollars—she thought he might at least have taken the morning off.

"This Antarctic thing is almost a wrap," Philip was saying, still explaining why he wouldn't be available. "I've wanted it for so long that it has almost become a habit. One of the directors from the university is coming up today for some meetings, and I don't want to miss them."

Rebecca didn't respond.

"Come on, Becky!" he pleaded. "You can see my point. I'll try to get off early; that's the best I can do."

She smiled apologetically. "I'm sorry. I shouldn't have expected you to drop everything and put your life on hold."

"I wouldn't mind putting everything on hold. But I can't do it until this afternoon."

They drove to the Painted Sands, where she quickly threw her things together and loaded them into Philip's car.

At the office, the manager, a skinny man with a shock of white hair clipped into a tight flattop, began to give her trouble. She had paid a week's rent in advance, and he refused to refund her the unused portion of her money.

"You should have made better plans," he said, attempting to stare her down from behind a pair of thick, black-rimmed glasses.

"Excuse me a moment," Philip interrupted, stepping up to the desk.

The manager eyed him, as if he recognized Philip but couldn't place his face.

"I'm a reporter for Channel 6," Philip continued. "If you don't give this woman an immediate refund, I'm going to call a camera crew in here, and we're going to tape every fire-code violation, every piece of trash, every dripping faucet, every cockroach and every bedbug crawling across every unmade bed in this place. Then I'm going to make sure that that tape is run every night for a week."

"You can't do that," the manager protested. "I've got rights."

Philip indicated Rebecca. "So does she. Pay now or pay later; it's up to you."

The manager regarded Philip contemptuously. "I'll pay her a refund," he said at last. "But it isn't because of you and your blackmail. I've got to make my books balance. I'm having trouble with my accountant."

"That's better than having trouble with me," Philip said, watching as the manager repaid Rebecca.

Rebecca followed in her rental car as Philip led her along crowded city streets. He drove a roundabout route that included a gratuitous stop at the police station. After trailing him along a particularly long stretch of straight road through a residential area, Rebecca was certain that no one was following. She flashed her lights in a prearranged signal, and Philip drove quickly to his condominium complex near the center of the city.

It was an enormous, sprawling collection of pink buildings, white trim, green lawns, and shimmering blue pools. Philip drove through the maze of the parking lot and finally parked under a long, shaded awning. Rebecca pulled in beside him.

"Very fancy," she remarked, eyeing the rows of towering palms that surrounded the complex. Tall olive trees and spruces provided generous shade to the grounds.

"Mine's just around the corner," he said. He opened her trunk, removed her suitcase, and led her along a narrow walkway to a unit at the rear of the complex. He opened the door, and they entered.

Rebecca was immediately taken by the condo's spacious airiness. A small foyer floored in peach-colored tile opened onto a wide living room carpeted a light blue. Sunlight spilled into the room through wide windows and long panels of pebbled glass that bordered the front door. A sensible arrangement of expensive-looking furniture contributed to the room's open feeling. Through an arched entryway on a side wall, she could just make out the white countertops of the kitchen.

"You'll be upstairs," Philip said, turning up a split-level staircase. She followed, her hand sliding up a decorative wrought-iron balustrade. Turning the corner at the landing, she noticed the fan-shaped, stained-glass window over the front door. The entire home was drenched in understated affluence.

The bedroom matched the rest of the home in its simple elegance. "You can sleep here," Philip told her, laying the suitcase on his bed. "I'll stay on the couch." He eyed her thoughtfully. "Unless, of course, you'd like another arrangement."

She smiled and said, "I think the original plan will be just fine."

He pointed out the adjoining bathroom and the enormous walk-in closet. "If it's mine, it's yours. Feel free to use anything you need."

"You've got a beautiful home," Rebecca remarked, standing in front of a floor-to-ceiling window that overlooked a shimmering pool. She found herself glancing quickly about the room, searching for evidence of another woman.

"Don't let it impress you," Philip said modestly. "In Phoenix condos are a dime a dozen."

"Maybe I should think of moving here," she mused.

"Maybe you should." He eyed her for a moment and arched his eyebrows. "For the moment it looks like you have."

"Don't go getting any ideas," she said, though her mind was full of them.

''No ideas?'' He crossed to her. ''What fun would that be?'' He slipped his arms around her waist. The warm sun cascaded over her through the tall window.

''It might keep us out of trouble.''

His face drew nearer hers. ''Trouble is my middle name,'' he whispered; then his lips brushed hers.

His touch sent waves of pleasure pulsing through her. His lips brushed hers again, as lightly as they had the first time, but his arms pulled her closer with unyielding strength.

Gone were Rebecca's memories of lonely nights, and vanished were her doubts about spending too much time together. She felt only intense, exquisite emotion. Her hands slid under his arms, up his back, and over his shoulders. His lips pressed against hers. Rebecca lost herself in their kiss.

The pressure of Philip's arms eased, and he pulled away slowly. ''I've always loved you,'' he said. His eyes were wide and blue and so very clear.

She knew that he was telling the truth. No man could fake the longing that had been in his kiss. Nor could she have faked hers. She wanted to tell him how she felt, that she loved him, but something, some deep fear of another abandonment stopped her. Instead, she looked away, embarrassed. ''I'd really like to change my clothes and put on some makeup,'' she said.

In that instant it disappeared. The longing, the desire, and the love in Philip's eyes vanished. A mask seemed to descend over his face that disguised his emotions. She had hurt him. Suddenly, more than ever, Rebecca needed to tell him the truth about her love, but for now the time was gone.

"I've got to make some calls," he said, excusing himself.

She fumbled through her things for a fresh change of clothes, chastising herself the entire time. Why was she unable to tell Philip how she felt about him? Deep down, she knew the answer. Her natural parents had abandoned her; then the Browns had been killed. Nothing, it seemed, was permanent, and she was so afraid of losing again.

Tears welled in her eyes as she slowly unpacked her things. Would she ever find the courage to fall in love again?

Chapter Seven

Rebecca gritted her teeth and inserted another spool of microfilm into the viewer. She was in the periodicals room of the Phoenix City Library, seated at the end of a long table, on top of which were several microfilm readers, arrayed in line like a rank of soldiers.

The automatic spooling mechanism whirred as she pressed her finger against the start button. For a moment only the fuzzy white field of the screen met her gaze; then suddenly the photographed pages of a newspaper began rolling lazily across the screen. She yanked her finger from the start button and pushed slow rewind until she arrived at the first frame.

The headlines of the *Maricopa Daily Informer* filled the viewer. The date below the masthead showed the paper to be just over five weeks old. Rebecca's eyes roamed the index for the obituary listing.

Locating the page, she pressed the scan button on the machine's console and watched silently as the paper scrolled lazily across the screen, one page at a time.

She lifted her finger from the scan button as she neared the obituary page, and manually advanced the film through the reader one frame at a time. Two turns later the death notices rolled onto the screen.

She quickly noted the names and dates of death of two

prominent valley residents whose names were listed, along with short biographies, near the upper-left corner of the page. Both were older men who had left behind considerable lists of survivors in addition to substantial business holdings. The information noted, she pressed the scan button once again and scrolled forward.

The pages of the paper once again slid across the screen, revealing the remainder of the day's news, as well as a lengthy section of classified ads. She watched without interest as the columns of black print slipped past.

Already the list she had compiled contained seventeen names. At the rate she was going, it would top one hundred by lunchtime. Attempting to locate her father by contacting the personal representative for each estate would require hours. Worse, there was no guarantee that her father's name was even on the list.

She battled the sense of hopelessness that tempted her to turn off the viewer and simply walk away. She knew that her labors held only a slim chance for locating her father's identity, but it was a chance she was determined to take. It was her only chance.

The thick black headlines of another issue of the *Informer* rolled onto the screen, and she stopped scanning.

Each roll of microfilm held two weeks' worth of newspapers. She had already searched through two spools, and her reaction to seeing another front page was automatic. Once again she located the index, then scanned forward to the obituary page.

The edgy sense of anticipation she had felt upon first entering the library had completely vanished. The motor inside the viewer whirred monotonously. Knowing that

Philip was enjoying a normal day at work aroused an angry feeling of jealousy in Rebecca. She stared blankly at the pages moving across the screen. Would it have been asking too much for a few hours of his help?

She let her fingers slide from the scan button and faced the screen dejectedly. The film had stopped, exposing three quarters of one page, and one quarter of the following, which appeared to be an advertisement for a grocery store. She noted sullenly that milk was cheaper in Phoenix than in LA, or at least it had been cheaper five weeks ago.

It was impossible, she realized. The task of sifting through obituaries in the hopes of locating her father was simply too enormous to take on by herself. She thought of Philip and smiled ruefully. Even two people wouldn't be able to cope with the volume of names and phone calls.

She slumped in her seat, facing the screen. There had to be a better way, she thought. The microfilm reader stared back at her. She had been among the first patrons through the library's doors that morning and was still alone in the room. She glanced at the big round clock on the far wall and scowled; the deadline for probate of the will was only slightly more than twelve hours away.

She rested her hands on the edge of the table. Her father, she was certain, had lived in Phoenix. But when had he died? According to Philip, probate could last anywhere from days to years. If she could just narrow the time frame down to within a couple of weeks, she could easily compile a list of names from the obituary pages and learn which estates were still in probate.

She glanced at the long list of names she had made. Without knowing an approximate date of her father's death, she was simply foraging in the dark. For all she knew, her father had died a year ago, and Tipton and Pepper had been working on the case ever since.

She slid the tablet with the list of names to the side of the microfilm reader. Trying to find her father through the papers was as good as useless. If only she could somehow find the identities of the clients for whom Tipton and Pepper were working!

They had tried the LAPD before leaving Philip's house but had received no new information. The Pinal County sheriff's office had given the same tight-lipped response. A final call to Philip's old acquaintances at KNXT had also yielded nothing.

Rebecca sighed. The microfilm reader faced her, tempting her to resume her futile search of obituary listings. She rewound the spool and returned it to the duty librarian, then walked upstairs to the library's lobby and settled in a comfortable chair to think.

Long, tinted windows faced a wide lawn that bordered Central Avenue. Traffic rolled smoothly along the corridor, the morning rush hour long since past.

With no hope of obtaining information regarding Tipton's client, Rebecca turned her attention to Pepper. Her lips twisted in disgust. Even thinking of the man was unpleasant. He was as callous, rude, and slovenly as anyone she had ever met. She didn't enjoy the prospect of doing business with him.

Still, she realized, he was the only direct link to the identity of her father. Or maybe, she thought, not so direct. By his own admission, he was working for someone who didn't want Rebecca found—perhaps a relative or friend of her father. Whatever the case, he had been willing to pay her fifty thousand dollars to give up her search.

She gazed absently at the traffic on Central Avenue. Suddenly sprinklers popped up from the lawn in front of the library. Long jets of water sprayed circles over the green grass.

Pepper was being paid to keep her from finding her father. She thought of the battered little car he drove and the dirty, frayed clothes he wore. He obviously wasn't having much success as a private detective. She remembered his brusque, churlish way and smiled to herself. His personality certainly was no help.

Then an idea occurred to her, an idea that was so simple she almost burst out laughing. She knew how she could find her father's identity, and the plan had nothing to do with prolonged, futile searches through old newspapers. How could she have overlooked it? She would pay Pepper for the information. She would pay him fifty thousand dollars.

She fumbled quickly through her purse for some change and hurried to a phone in the red-tiled entry foyer. She dialed Pepper's number and waited. After several rings an answering machine kicked in.

She was a bit surprised that Pepper himself didn't answer. She had expected he would be waiting beside the phone for her call, ready to drop his offer to forty thousand if she would sign his contract.

She left a message that she wanted to speak with him

and would be trying to contact him later. She hung up, anxious to tell Philip of her plan.

She searched through her purse for more coins but didn't have enough change for another call. Momentarily stumped, she spied the circulation desk. A large placard over the end of the counter read FINES.

Trying desperately to contain her excitement, she hurried to the fines counter. An elderly woman wearing steel-rimmed glasses and a string of white pearls watched with narrowed eyes as she approached.

"Could you change this dollar?" Rebecca asked, laying the bill atop the oaken counter. "I need to make a phone call."

The elderly woman eyed her without moving. "We don't make change for phone calls," she said sharply.

Rebecca was taken aback by the woman's curt manner. "I would appreciate it if you could make an exception." She smiled warmly, knowing that a smile was more likely to get her what she wanted than a frown. "I know you must be pestered all the time for change, but this is something of an emergency."

The woman eyed her as if deep in thought.

Rebecca glanced quickly around the almost vacant library and lowered her voice. "I promise to keep it a secret," she said as a joke.

What might have been a smile crossed the librarian's lips and as quickly disappeared. She opened a small drawer. "We get so many coming in here wanting change, and not just for phone calls, either, but for parking meters and those video machines at the arcade across the street." She shook her head, silently disparaging those who would take advantage of the fines window at a public library, and counted four quarters into her palm.

"I appreciate this," Rebecca said, handing her the bill.

The librarian snatched the dollar and laid the quarters atop the counter, again counting them to herself, her lips moving thinly as she did. Then she slid them to Rebecca, one at a time, counting them aloud, "Twenty-five, fifty, seventy-five . . . one dollar." She slid the final quarter across the counter.

The intricate ceremony would never have taken place, Rebecca knew, had she not been in a hurry.

The phantom smile once again crossed the librarian's lips. She had done her job well. The books would balance tonight.

Rebecca gathered the coins and forced a smile. "Thanks again," she said and walked quickly back to the phone.

Philip answered on the second ring.

"I know how we can find my father," she said.

"Did you get a break on the papers?"

"That's useless," she answered, explaining why. "But I think I have a foolproof plan for learning my father's identity."

Philip sounded interested. She could almost see him leaning forward, pinching his lip.

"It's so simple, you'll kick yourself for not thinking of it," she told him.

"I've suffered worse," Philip said impatiently. "Tell me."

Rebecca took a breath. "Pepper was willing to pay me

fifty thousand to give up the search for my father, right? So I simply agree to the deal.'' She paused dramatically.

''How will that help?'' Philip asked, sounding incredulous.

Rebecca smiled. ''It will give me fifty thousand dollars to spend on information. You've seen the car Pepper drives. You've seen his clothes. His line of work obviously isn't paying him too well.''

''So you think he'll turn over for the fifty thousand dollars?''

''Don't you?''

She was met with silence.

''Don't you think he'd tell me for fifty thousand dollars?'' she asked.

Philip laughed. ''I can't answer. I'm too busy kicking myself. You're brilliant.''

''You sound surprised.''

''That's only because I am.''

''Well,'' she sniffed, ''you're not the only one in the world with a brain.''

He laughed again. ''I know, but I like to think so. By the way, I've been trying to contact Pepper all morning, and all I've been getting is his answering machine.''

Rebecca let his brain comment slide. ''I tried to call him too,'' she said. ''I'm surprised he isn't waiting for our call.''

''I was sure he would be,'' Philip agreed. ''You're right about one thing, though—he doesn't seem to be making his fortune as a private investigator. It's a sure thing that he's not working on another case.''

He was interrupted momentarily by someone in the

office. "Sorry," he said, coming back on the line. "Of course, there's always the possibility that Pepper is sitting right there in his office, listening to our calls with a big smile on his face, happy because he's making us sweat."

Rebecca had to agree with this possibility. Pepper liked being in control.

"Look," Philip said, "why don't you come on back to the station? I have a few more things to wrap up here; then we'll take off for lunch."

Rebecca accepted his offer.

"Oh, and one more thing," he added. "You're buying."

Before she could respond, he had hung up.

Chapter Eight

Rebecca knew something had happened as soon as she stepped from her car in the station's parking lot. Philip was already out the front door and running toward her.

"We've got to move," he called. "It looks like Pepper is dead."

Rebecca felt herself grow weak. "Dead?" she asked. "How?"

"We monitor police frequencies, and we just got a report of a car overturned in a canal on the east side. They ran a make on the plate, and it was Pepper's."

Her mind was in a whirl. Both investigators who'd been working the case had been murdered.

Philip placed a hand on her shoulder. "We've got to get out there," he said. "A camera crew is on the way." He led her to his car, and they pulled into traffic.

They rode in silence down the Squaw Peak freeway. Rebecca was lost in thought. So far she had been approached by two men who had claimed to know her father's identity, and both had been murdered. "I'm scared," she said at last.

Philip glanced at her, his face set. "Tipton and Pepper both knew you, and both were working for people who knew your father. Pepper admitted that there were certain people who didn't want you found. The killer must be one of them."

"I could be next," Rebecca pointed out, her voice barely a whisper.

Philip was quiet for a second. "You don't know anything more about this case today than you did on the night you met Tipton."

"The killer can't know that for sure," she replied. She bit at her bottom lip. Suddenly she wanted Philip to stop the car. She wanted to jump out and run away. Back to California. Back to a week ago, before any of this had happened.

Philip sped down the highway and merged with a line of cars that were heading eastward on the Superstition Freeway.

"We'll be there in a few minutes," he said. "We should be able to get some answers."

They drove in silence the few remaining miles to the scene of the accident. Rebecca spotted the cordon of police cars long before she caught sight of the overturned vehicle.

Philip pulled off the road and parked on a dirt strip access road that edged the canal. A blue-and-white Channel 6 mini-van was parked several feet ahead, its enormous dish antenna projecting awkwardly from the roof.

Philip rushed to meet the remote camera team, who were finishing preparations for taping the scene. Rebecca followed him but couldn't keep her eyes off the upturned car in the ditch.

Its four wheels poked incongruously upward at the blue sky. It was jammed tightly between the walls of the canal.

The front end had sunk slightly lower than the rear, and the back license plate was exposed, along with a patch of faded green bodywork. Water lapped around the edges of the rusted undercarriage.

She knew that it was Pepper's even without seeing the rest of the car. She could imagine him down there, stuck beneath the steering wheel, pinned in the wreckage, unable to swim free. The thought sent shudders down her spine.

"There isn't too much to tell," Philip said, coming up beside her. "A couple of kids found it. They were out here skipping rocks. The car's pretty well hidden from view by the canal banks. No telling when it went in." He turned his attention to the car. "A diver is supposed to be arriving for a look."

"It's so awful," Rebecca said. "To be killed that way. Drowned. Trapped inside his car with no hope of escape."

"We can't be certain that it was murder," Philip cautioned. "Cars run into these ditches all the time."

Rebecca looked at him, then at the mini-van. "If it's so standard," she said, "then why the news crew?"

He shrugged. "The timing is a little too coincidental."

A police van drew up to the scene, and an officer carrying scuba gear jumped out. He walked briskly to the edge of the canal, nodding as he was briefed by the officer in charge. He slipped into his gear and stepped off the bank into the canal.

"Now we'll find out who was in there," Philip said, leading her to the bank.

The camera crew was there, too, poised over the water,

recording the movements of the diver under the surface. He reappeared after a few minutes, pushed his face mask back, and spit out his regulator. "One body," he shouted to the officer in charge. "White male." He indicated that he would search a section of the canal bottom and again disappeared beneath the surface.

Rebecca felt Philip's hand tighten on her shoulder.

The diver surfaced several feet downstream. "The current's pretty strong here," he said. "Anyone out of the car would have been swept away and caught up in one of the sluice gates farther down."

Again Rebecca shuddered. "How can they be so insensitive?"

"They work with it every day," Philip responded. He gestured to the camera crew, then followed them as they moved along the canal bank toward the diver emerging from the canal.

Rebecca returned to Philip's car. She had seen enough. She sat in the front seat with the door open, watching the newsmen surround the diver.

Philip was trotting toward her. "They're sending a crane to pull the car out of the canal," he said. "I think we ought to stick around just in case they find anything."

Rebecca nodded but didn't speak.

Philip squatted beside the car and faced her. "I know that you're scared, but I don't think you need to be. Pepper probably rolled his car sometime last night. These canal access roads are supposed to be off-limits, but people use them all the time as shortcuts." He patted her leg reassuringly.

An enormous orange-and-white crane rumbled onto the

scene, followed closely by a flatbed tow truck. After a great deal of arm waving and traffic directing on the part of the officer in charge, the trucks maneuvered into position on the canal bank.

"They'll pull it up with the crane and cart it off on the truck," Philip explained.

The crane planted its outriggers firmly for support, then turned its boom. A pair of hooks dangled from the winch cable.

The operator jumped from the cab and walked to the bank. He made a quick survey of the situation, called to the tow-truck driver, then climbed behind a maze of control levers in the winch cabin.

The tow-truck driver jumped squarely onto the center of the upturned chassis. He quickly placed the hooks under the rear axle and scrambled back to his truck. The news crew taped the entire procedure.

"This is some good footage," Philip said, watching the film crew work. "This will work in well."

The crane's winch growled to life, and the cable grew taut under the weight of the car. The diesel engine roared and blew a cloud of black smoke through its pipes. Slowly, almost immeasurably at first, Pepper's battered green car emerged from the canal. The rear end appeared, then the rear side panels. Water gushed from the open front-seat windows and streamed from the front grill as the car was lifted free of the canal. Rebecca thought she saw Pepper's lifeless body face downward against the steering wheel.

The crane rotated slowly, and Pepper's car sailed through the air, nose down, until it hovered over dry land. With a loud clang the winch motor reversed and began lowering the car to the ground.

It stood on its front bumper for a moment, suspended by the steel cable; then the boom retracted slowly, and the operator paid out cable. By degrees Pepper's car descended onto its four wheels. More water dripped from its chassis when it was at last flat on the ground.

The camera crew surrounded the car but was quickly waved off by the officer in charge. "Give us some room to work," he said. He and another officer on the scene made a quick inspection of the car. He turned to the tow-truck operator and said, "We're going to have to wait for the coroner." His partner draped a blanket over the body in the car.

Philip and Rebecca approached from the passenger side. "It doesn't look like it was run off the road," Philip noted.

Rebecca agreed. The only damage to the car appeared to have been caused by the concrete canal banks.

"Are those bullet holes?" Philip asked suddenly, pointing to a pair of holes in the passenger door.

Rebecca peered intently at the door panel while Philip instructed the camera crew to take close-ups of the holes.

She leaned against him. He circled her shoulders with his arms. "It's going to work out all right," he said. "Nothing will happen to you."

She listened to his words and wanted to believe him, but she was afraid. Afraid that she would be next.

A light-blue mini-van arrived, the medical examiner's insignia on its side.

"We'll get some information now," Philip said.

Rebecca felt her lower lip trembling with fear. "I think we already know what happened."

Philip patted her shoulder and moved to intercept the ME.

Rebecca watched as the examiner peeled the wet blanket from Pepper's still form and made a quick examination.

Philip spoke to him shortly, then returned to her side. "Gunshot," he said. "A medium or large-caliber weapon."

Rebecca felt herself begin to cry. Pepper had been awful, but he hadn't deserved this.

Philip stroked her shoulder. After several seconds he said, "I think Pepper's disappearance might help us find your father."

She sniffed and dabbed at her tears without responding.

"I'll be back in a minute," he said. He let go of her and strode to the camera crew, who were positioned beside the tow truck, waiting for one last shot. He made some notes on a pad, then grabbed a microphone that the sound man handed him. The camera was pointed in his direction, and he began to speak.

"We run three news programs in the evening," Philip explained as he and Rebecca were returning to the studio. "One at five o'clock, one at six, and a final broadcast at ten." He eyed her significantly. "If Todd Blanchard, the news director, agrees to let me do it, I think we have a chance of getting your story on at six."

"Mine?"

"Don't act so surprised. You're the perfect subject for

a news story. I wasn't bluffing when I told Pepper we'd run a piece on you. We have a segment we run every Tuesday and Thursday at six o'clock called Crime Stoppers. We examine a crime and ask viewers to call our CrimeLine number if they have any information.''

''You want to put me on a Crime Stoppers spot?'' Rebecca asked.

''Blanchard has to agree,'' he responded. ''But it's a perfect story. You were approached by two private investigators who claimed to have information about the identity of your father. You were led to believe that learning his identity could mean a great deal of money to you. Now, both of those investigators are dead, and you have only a matter of hours to learn who he was before you're cut out of your rightful share of an inheritance.''

''I don't know,'' Rebecca said, listening to Philip unveil his plan. ''It makes me sound so greedy.''

''I won't do anything with this unless you want me to,'' Philip promised. ''I can't even say for sure whether Blanchard will let it fly, but I honestly see it, at this point, as our only chance to learn the identity of your father.''

''*Our* only chance?'' Rebecca asked.

''We're in this together, aren't we?''

''It seems to be going that way,'' she said, glad that he was so committed to the story. She mulled his proposition over in silence for several seconds.

''I can't understand why you're so worried about the money angle,'' Philip said, intruding on her thoughts. ''No one would hold it against you for being interested in claiming an inheritance. This man may be your true father, but you never even knew him.'' He regarded her thoughtfully, then returned his attention to the road. "You've always considered the Browns to be your parents. This shouldn't change that."

"You're right," she said, picturing her father's face. "Tom Brown will always be my father. I don't even know who this man is." She hesitated. "But I need to."

"But the man who meant the most to you," Philip persisted, "was the one who raised you. Our viewers will recognize that fact. You have only a few hours left to claim your inheritance. Maybe by showing your story we'll get some action. Someone had to have hired Tipton. If they're watching, they'll call."

"That's a big 'if,' " she said.

He nodded. "You're right. And there's another big 'if.' "

"Blanchard?"

"What he says goes." He shrugged as if to dismiss the thought. "We run promos throughout the afternoon on all the major valley radio stations, highlighting what we'll be covering on the evening news. Promos for the five o'clock news have to be ready by three, those for the six o'clock broadcast by four. I think we have enough time to get some promos ready for the six o'clock show."

Rebecca said, "It seems like a lot of work to go through just for me."

"Then you don't think you're worth it?" Philip asked rhetorically. "I do. In any event, for as long as I've known you, I've had a sense that you would never be truly happy unless you knew who your. . . ." He hesitated for a moment, searching for the proper words. "Unless you knew who your biological parents were."

She smiled as she watched him drive. "You're right. I'll tell you something else, something I've never told anyone. I've always hoped that I would find some Irish blood in my background so I could have a genuine reason to celebrate St. Patrick's Day."

Philip laughed. "Well, now's your chance." He glanced at her and smiled. "I've always suspected that you might be Irish," he said. "With your temper and all."

"What is that supposed to mean?"

"Don't get mad," he responded with a laugh. "Of course, a true Irishman would never need a reason for celebrating St. Patrick's Day."

Back at the station, Rebecca was amazed by the amount of activity in the newsroom. Teletypes clattered, people ran back and forth, and television screens seemed to flicker everywhere. Nothing stood still for very long, except her.

For fifteen minutes she waited while Philip met with the news director, alternately thumbing through an old copy of a sports magazine she had found in his bottom desk drawer and staring at the bank of clocks on the far wall, which displayed times from all the world's time zones. All the while, she wondered whether her story would make it onto the six o'clock news.

Finally Philip reappeared. "We're on," he said. But before Rebecca could react, he added, "We can't air at six, though. It's ten o'clock or nothing. Blanchard's going to run the piece on Pepper at six, but your half will have to wait until later."

''It's our only chance,'' she said, standing. She wanted to hug him.

He glanced over his shoulder and lowered his voice to a conspiratorial whisper. ''Take a seat.''

Rebecca did as she was told, eyeing Philip curiously.

''Nobody can know that there's anything between us,'' he cautioned. ''I told Blanchard that you'd called me because you'd come here from LA and you'd seen my report on the spraying at El Toro's and you thought I might be able to help you. If he had suspected that there was anything personal, he would have spiked this.''

He glanced at his watch. ''I've got to go pass the word to the crew who were out there with us today when Pepper's car was being recovered.''

Rebecca was baffled. ''What word?''

Philip smiled. ''How soon they forget.'' He leaned forward. ''I had my arm around you.'' He straightened. ''They won't say anything. I'll be back in a minute. We've got some work to do.''

Philip returned momentarily. ''I want to work on the promos first,'' he said, plopping a large yellow notepad atop his desk. He glanced around and borrowed a chair from a nearby desk. ''We always run a few promo pieces for the ten o'clock news between six and nine. I'm going to script this out quickly and have our ten o'clock anchor, Paulette Ruiz, record it; then we'll get to taping your spot.''

He began to write furiously, quickly covering several lines on one of the yellow sheets. ''I've got three versions here,'' he said. ''Here's the first: Find out how the murder of Tucson Private Eye Delbert Tipton ties in with a young woman's trip to Phoenix, her search for a missing will, and the killing of a second investigator.''

He raised his eyebrows. ''Well?''

''Dramatic,'' Rebecca said.

''I hope so,'' Philip answered. ''The whole point of these promotions is to draw viewer attention. Of course, we're aiming these at a specific viewer—the one who hired Tipton, the one who wants you found.''

Rebecca nodded. ''If they're listening, they'll hear it.''

Philip looked at the pad. He seemed to be thinking for a moment; then he shrugged. ''The other two are pretty much the same. I made a point of mentioning Tipton's name in each. Paulette will read them over and pick the one she's most comfortable with; then she'll add a few other headlines and put it on a cassette tape. The tapes will be distributed to the radio stations we work with, and with a little luck the people we're looking for will hear them and watch our broadcast tonight.''

''It seems like we can't miss,'' Rebecca said.

Philip shook his head. ''It isn't that rosy. By putting the radio spots on after six o'clock, we miss the primary drive time when people are heading home from work. Spots that air after six o'clock are much less effective than those that air in the late afternoon. Of course, we always plug the major stories for the ten o'clock news during the six o'clock broadcast.''

''Then we'll just have to hope that whoever we're looking for makes a habit of watching the Channel 6 news,'' Rebecca said.

Philip smiled widely. ''We're rated first in that time

slot.'' He glanced down at the yellow pad on his desk. ''I've got to get this over to Paulette. I'll be right back.''

Rebecca sat quietly at Philip's desk, watching the bustle of activity in the newsroom. She spotted the anchor of the six o'clock news. She looked older in person than she did on TV.

Philip returned with a smile. ''Everything's going according to schedule,'' he said. ''We'll record your spot over there.'' He nodded toward one of the glass-walled conference rooms.

Feeling vain, she asked, ''Would it be possible for me to rush home and change my clothes? I never expected to be on TV when I left the library this morning.''

Philip grinned. ''No, that wouldn't be possible. But don't worry, you look beautiful just the way you are.''

Rebecca smiled at the compliment, though she knew that her white slacks and orange pullover were hardly suited for television. ''You'd better be careful,'' she said. ''Someone might hear.''

''I'll keep it in mind. There's a full-length mirror just inside of that alcove.'' He tilted his head toward a wall across the room. ''If it will set your nerves a little more at ease, you can step around and make sure that your hair is in place before we tape.''

''I think I'll do that,'' she said.

She returned to find Philip standing beside his desk. ''We're ready,'' he told her.

Rebecca eyed the cameraman inside the glass walls of the conference room. He was the same one who had covered the retrieval of Pepper's car. Like Philip, he was calm and relaxed. This was just another job for him.

''Nervous?'' Philip asked.

She nodded. ''Very.''

He smiled at her. She could have used his comforting arm on her shoulders now, but that was not to be. ''Just be yourself,'' he said. ''I'm tight with Jay, the cameraman. He'll make sure that you look good. And we won't have to put on an act for him, either. He knows about us.''

Rebecca wondered what he'd meant by that last comment, but she didn't ask. Instead, she said, ''What if I stumble all over my words?''

Philip shrugged. ''We'll just tape another take.'' He gestured politely with his hands. ''After you.''

Rebecca walked slowly toward the conference room, each step increasing the anxiety she was feeling. By the time she was through the door and settled in a seat under a large mural of a Hopi pueblo, her fear was a cold ball in the pit of her stomach, and her mouth was as dry as the sands of the Sahara.

Philip and Jay conferred quickly over the placement of lights, and the interview began.

''This won't take too long,'' Philip said, taking a seat opposite her. ''If you begin to feel uncomfortable, or if for any reason you want the camera to be turned off, just tell us, and it's done.''

Rebecca smiled self-consciously. ''I'm getting hungry. What if my stomach growls?''

''We'll definitely leave that in,'' Philip said.

''We like the human element,'' Jay added.

She glanced at him and was suddenly very aware of the camera aimed at her. ''What about you, Philip?'' she asked. She nodded at the camera positioned on a tripod just over his right shoulder. "Aren't you going to be taped?"

"Do you think I'm camera shy?" he asked with a laugh.

Jay laughed, too. "Not this guy," he said.

"I'll get a few cuts," Philip said. "I'm asking the questions now, and we're taping your responses. When we're finished, Jay will take a few shots of me repeating the questions. Then we'll head into the booth and edit it up so that it all looks like one uninterrupted piece of work."

Rebecca nodded. "Then I guess we're all ready."

The interview lasted less than five minutes. Philip skillfully guided Rebecca through the events of the past days. His questions were focused and to the point. When she was finished, Rebecca realized that the entire affair had been condensed into a series of high points: her adoption, Tipton's murder, Pepper's disappearance, and the deadline for claiming her inheritance. By the time it was edited, she knew, the interview would air for less than one minute.

"We're going to tape my spots now," Philip said. "Then we'll head to the booth to put it all together."

He remained seated, and Jay shifted the camera to point at him. Philip checked his notepad and said, "I jotted down a few quotes as you spoke. The questions I ask now won't be the same as the ones I originally asked you, but when we're finished with the editing, no one will ever be able to tell." He glanced at Jay. "Ready?"

"All set."

Philip nodded. Suddenly a serious expression crossed his face. "And you'd never heard of either of these men?" He sat quietly for a few seconds, then nodded his head, as if understanding some silent response. "What help have you been able to obtain from the police?" he asked next. He was again silent for a moment; then his face broke into a wide grin. "That ought to do it," he said, standing up.

Jay turned to Rebecca. "Bet you didn't know how to make an interview for TV news until today, right?"

Rebecca couldn't help but smile. Seeing Philip asking questions into empty space had been almost comical. "I didn't realize that it was so staged."

"I wouldn't exactly call it staged," Philip said as he helped Jay break down camera and sound gear. "Newsmen who work in print have the opportunity to present a story in a way that they believe will best portray the truth. Given the same set of facts, no two newsmen will write the same story.

"I don't see why it should be any different for television journalists. It's too simple to turn a camera on someone and record their words and say, 'There, that's the story.' My job is to clarify an event, make it accessible to everyone. If it requires several takes and an hour of editing to get that clarity, I'll spend the time. I owe it to my audience."

Rebecca understood his point, but the actual strategy behind the composition of the story seemed somehow devious to her. Viewers would have the impression that events took place during the interview that hadn't actually occurred. "For instance, your question about the police," she said. "You never asked about that."

Philip finished coiling a microphone cord and handed it to Jay. "The interview isn't the story," he said. "The story is the story." He grabbed his notepad and pen. "True, I never asked you about the police, but you brought it up in response to another question. I feel that the lack of help you've received from the police is an important point, and I intend for viewers to see this as well."

Jay was standing beside the door, camera in one hand and a steel case containing sound equipment in the other. "If we're done here," he said, "I'm going to head out to dinner. I'm pulling City Watch tonight, and I don't want to go hungry like I did last time."

"Take off," Philip invited, "and eat something for me."

"You'll probably want this." Jay handed him the video he'd just taped.

"I think it will come in handy." Philip turned to Rebecca. "City Watch is the on-call staff. Jay was working it one night when a call came through about a fire in an ammo plant near Tucson. He's never let anyone forget that he missed dinner that night."

"Speaking of food," Rebecca said, "I'm beginning to notice that we missed lunch today."

"Things have been moving pretty quickly, haven't they?" Philip hefted the videotape in his hand. "It'll take a little while to edit and dub this. I always do my own pieces myself. Anyway, we want it perfect for the ten o'clock news."

"About how long do you think it will take?" she asked.

Philip looked at her, then the tape, then again at her. He shrugged. "Let's find out. The booth is right outside that door. I think we'll be having a late dinner tonight."

"Are you trying to starve me?"

"Just think how much better everything will taste when you finally get to eat. And don't worry," he added. "I'm buying."

"That will make it taste even better," Rebecca said with a laugh, and they headed for the editing booth.

Chapter Nine

The Arizona Steak Company was an exclusive restaurant disguised as a rural watering hole. The parking lot was crowded with expensive cars, and the patrons were dressed in the relaxed style that only true money can buy. Those who missed the more subtle signs, however, learned quickly that the Company didn't cater to just anyone.

Rebecca looked at the menu and thought her eyes would drop out of her head and roll across the floor. "You can't afford this," she said in a hoarse whisper.

Philip looked chagrined. "Why don't you just announce it to the whole restaurant? I don't think they heard you over in the corner booth."

"I didn't say it that loudly."

"Oh, really? That fake whisper of yours sounds like waves crashing on a rocky beach."

She glanced around, feeling guilty. The other diners in the restaurant ate their meals, oblivious to her conversation with Philip. "I just think that we could have gone somewhere a little less expensive," she said.

"I have never, ever, gone with a woman who was as concerned with money as you are."

"Well," Rebecca said smugly, "maybe if you had, you'd have more money to spend."

"Spend on what? I've got money to spend, and I want to spend it. Now you're telling me I shouldn't."

"I'm not saying you shouldn't spend it," she corrected. "I just don't think that you should spend it on dinner."

"Well, it's too late now, because we're already here."

"I'll just have a salad," she said.

"Fine," Philip agreed, biting off the word. "Fine, just a salad, and maybe some milk in a dirty glass. Anything at all. Just make sure that you don't enjoy yourself."

"I don't need a big, fancy meal to enjoy myself."

"What do you need?" Philip asked wryly. "An argument?"

Rebecca crossed her hands atop the menu. "I'll just wait for the waiter," she said. She turned to survey the restaurant but watched Philip from the corner of her eye. It wasn't nice to tease him, she knew. But sometimes it was fun.

Soon a waiter appeared. He was wearing a red-and-white-checked cowboy shirt and a pair of blue jeans.

Philip ordered. "I'd like the T-bone," he said. He glanced at Rebecca. "And a dinner salad."

"All right," the waiter said, writing the ticket. "Anything to drink while you wait?"

Philip eyed Rebecca, then said, "I don't think that will be necessary."

"Just a minute," Rebecca interrupted before the waiter could leave. "Could I see a wine list? And, as a matter of fact, I'm in the mood for something more than a salad. Could you make that two T-bones?" She smiled widely at the waiter.

The waiter returned her grin. ''Certainly,'' he said, making the corrections to the ticket. He flashed a quick, questioning glance at Philip. ''I'll be back with the wine list in a second.''

''Would you mind telling me what that was all about?'' Philip asked when he was gone. ''That guy must think I'm an idiot.''

''Serves you right.''

''Serves me right for what?''

''For trying to impress me by bringing me to a fancy restaurant you probably can't afford.''

''Then let's go get hamburgers.''

''We're already here.'' Philip shook his head, and Rebecca laughed. ''I'm only teasing,'' she said.

He smiled. ''I know. But if it's not asking too much, I'd like to get serious for a minute.''

He eyed her for a moment before continuing. ''I don't want to drag it all out of the closet again for another beating. Things didn't work out for us the first time, and I know that I was mostly to blame.'' He stopped for a moment to gauge her reaction.

Rebecca allowed him to continue without commenting.

He gazed at her in the silence, and though he said nothing, she could read the longing in his eyes.

''I'd like to try again,'' he said. ''That is, if you're willing.''

A familiar fear rose in Rebecca. If she gave her heart to him for the second time and it didn't work out, she didn't know if she would be able to stand the pain.

Philip's eyes peered into her soul. She felt him reading her mind.

"What makes you think it will work this time?" Rebecca asked. "I live in LA, and you live in Phoenix."

"It's not that far. We could see each other on weekends. It's only an hour by air." He watched her, trying to gauge her reaction. "Things change. I've changed. We never know what lies down the road." Rebecca could see desire and pain in his expression. "All I'm asking for is one more chance."

She hesitated for a moment before answering, unsure of her exact words but certain of her answer. "I'd like that," she said.

A wide smile crossed Philip's face. "Fantastic!"

Rebecca smiled too. His enthusiasm was flattering.

"The wine list you asked for," said the waiter who had appeared as if from thin air.

She took the list and quickly read through it. She tried not to concentrate on the prices but found it impossible to completely block them out. She finally settled on a Burgundy. The waiter voiced his agreement and disappeared for the bottle.

"Maybe we should be drinking champagne," Philip suggested, reaching across the table and clasping Rebecca's hands in his. "We're celebrating."

His hands were warm, and his eyes inviting. She felt as though she were in a trance. She'd shed her cocoon of fear and was wrapped in magic. Never before had she felt such love. This was the man with whom she wanted to spend forever.

The waiter returned with the wine and two glasses. The mood faded. Philip was forced to let go of Rebecca's hands. He watched the waiter pour the wine; then he turned back to Rebecca and smiled. Like a wonderful spell, the magic surrounded her once again.

Later, as they walked across the parking lot, Philip's hand slid around Rebecca's waist and pulled her close. She leaned against his strong body as his arm encircled her. When they arrived at his car, he said, "There's something I've been wanting to tell you."

"What's that?" Rebecca asked.

He turned her toward him and squeezed her tightly to his body. "This," he said.

His lips met hers, gently at first, then becoming more and more insistent. His grip tightened around her waist, his powerful arms clutching her as if he were afraid she might slip away. Rebecca responded with all her heart.

"Do you think we have a future?" he asked.

"I've always thought so."

"I hate to say it," Philip said, drawing away from her slowly, "but we've got to get back to the station."

Rebecca snuggled against his chest. "I hate to hear you say it."

"I want to make sure that Blanchard isn't demanding any changes in the piece," he said.

The drive back to the station passed too quickly for Rebecca. While she was alone in the car with Philip, she was on an island, a fabulous desert island inhabited by only two and sheltered from the grimmer aspects of life by shimmering reefs of pink coral.

But at the station she was quickly reminded of the reality that surrounded her.

"New word on Pepper," Philip reported, returning from a short meeting with Blanchard. "Those *were* bullet holes in his car. Thirty-eight. He was killed by a shot to the head. The police think he was driving along the access road when someone pulled up beside him and started shooting through the open passenger-side window."

"Do they have any suspects?" Rebecca asked.

"It's a good question." He picked up the videotape they'd made. "Nobody's saying." He seemed momentarily lost in thought. "I want to get this new information onto the tape. The writers will work it into the anchor's copy as well," he said, mostly to himself. He smiled at her. "Don't be scared. This is all going to be over tonight. Midnight's the time, remember. You're safe here."

She smiled back at him.

"I'd ask you to come to the booth with me, but it's liable to be crowded at this time of night. It shouldn't take too long."

"I'll read your magazine," Rebecca said, sliding the desk drawer open.

"If you find any food in there, don't eat it. It's rotten."

"Don't worry," she answered. "That expensive meal you bought me filled me up."

"I wish you'd stop thinking about money," he said as he left.

Sitting alone at his desk, Rebecca found it difficult to concentrate on the magazine. She found it difficult to concentrate on Philip. She found it difficult to concentrate on anything but the murders of Tipton and Pepper.

Two dead, and the identity of her father still a mystery. Even in the newsroom, with its lights and commotion, she felt like a hunted animal. Rebecca shuddered. The fact that she knew nothing was meaningless if the murderer suspected otherwise. He would track her down and kill her, just as he had the others.

Philip returned shortly. "It's all set," he said. "All we have to do is wait for the broadcast." He checked the clock on the wall. "I think we should stay here until it's over. We'll want to be available in case anyone calls the CrimeLine with information."

Rebecca agreed. "I'm scared, Philip."

He cast her a reassuring glance. "There's nothing to be afraid of," he said, gesturing to the crowded newsroom. "You have plenty of protection here. Anyway, it will all be over at midnight."

He was right, Rebecca knew. The murderer had undoubtedly intended that she never inherit under the will. She glanced at the clock. Slightly more than two hours remained until the twelve o'clock deadline.

"The murderer must realize that I could contest the will even if I didn't meet the deadline," she said.

"Let's just take things one step at a time," he advised.

"I feel like a target." The frightening image of the wet blanket draped over Pepper chilled her.

"We'll have our answer in less than half an hour. By then your spot will have been broadcast, and anyone interested in calling will have done so."

Philip stepped to a desk near his, pulled open the bottom drawer, and lifted out a mini TV. "Tony won't mind," he said, bending to plug it into an outlet on the floor.

He tuned in the station and adjusted the volume and the color. Then they settled down to watch the news.

Opening credits rolled by to the accompaniment of

orchestral music and an authoritative, male voice-over announcing "Channel 6 News at Ten." Fast cuts of places and events throughout Arizona filled the tiny screen. Finally the opening leader faded out. Rebecca leaned forward expectantly. The station broke to a commercial.

She slumped impatiently in her seat.

"We have to earn our money somehow," Philip said.

She smiled in spite of herself. She glanced absently at the row of clocks on the wall. "Do they pay by the hour?"

"It will be on soon enough," Philip assured her. "We always air local news first, followed by national, then sports and weather." He paused significantly. "When it's finally over, you may wish that it wasn't."

"You mean we might not get a call."

He shrugged. "It's our last chance to meet the deadline."

Rebecca glanced back at the TV in time to see Paulette Ruiz's face fade in. She began the newscast with a report on a tax scam that threatened to destroy the careers of several state legislators. The screen flipped to a videotaped report from the state capitol.

Rebecca watched without listening. So much depended on the following minutes. They had done all they could do. Now all she could do was hope.

"Here it is," Philip said, leaning forward attentively.

Rebecca's eyes were glued to the screen. Paulette was reading the introduction to Philip's piece. ". . . the murdered investigator may be tied to a bizarre mystery involving the killing of at least one other Arizona private investigator and the search for a lost heir. Philip Grant reports with tonight's Crime Stoppers report.''

The screen flipped to footage of Pepper's car being lifted from the canal. Philip's voice was dubbed over the scene. ''The mysterious death of private investigator Robert Pepper is only the latest chapter in a bizarre tale of murder and intrigue. . . .''

Suddenly Rebecca was watching herself. ''The story revolves around this woman, Rebecca Brown, a schoolteacher from Los Angeles.''

She examined her televised image with a critical eye. She looked heavier on the screen than she really was, and her nose seemed to shine. She wished she'd had a chance to fix her makeup.

She forced herself to concentrate on what was being said and not how she looked. Her interview with Philip ran almost exactly as they had edited it in the booth before going to dinner, though new information about the weapon used in Pepper's murder had been skillfully inserted. The segment concluded with Philip asking about police help and Rebecca answering that she had so far received very little.

Paulette's face returned to the screen, asking anyone with information to call the Channel 6 CrimeLine. A number flashed at the bottom of the screen.

''That's it,'' Philip announced as soon as it was over.

''You did a great job,'' Rebecca said sincerely.

''We had the whole thing sewed up in just under a minute,'' he said, obviously proud of the piece.

''Now we wait for phone calls.''

"There's the CrimeLine desk." Philip nodded toward a desk in the corner.

Rebecca tried to stifle the urge to move, wanting instead to appear calm and aloof, but she lost her battle with herself. "Maybe we should be there in case it rings," she suggested nervously.

Two men wearing T-shirts and carrying Styrofoam cups of coffee walked past, laughing loudly at a private joke.

Philip stood from his seat. "I think we would hear it from here," he said with a smile, "but I'm a little anxious myself."

As they crossed to the CrimeLine desk, the phone suddenly started to ring.

"Cross your fingers," Philip said, rushing to answer it. He snatched at the receiver. "CrimeLine."

He was silent for a second, then began answering the caller with simple, one-word responses. "Yes . . . right . . . right. . . ."

Rebecca watched, her heart pounding heavily, her palms suddenly moist.

Philip thanked the caller and hung up. "No go," he said. "He claimed the whole thing was a plot to help divide some money embezzled from a bank years ago. Just calling to be heard, I guess."

Rebecca's hopes crashed. She had never considered the possibility of crank callers.

They sat silently at the desk. Suddenly the phone rang again. Philip eyed it with cautious optimism. "Busy night," he said, answering it.

He listened to the voice on the other end and nodded

his head. "That's right," he said. Suddenly he was on his feet. He nodded a few more times and glanced at Rebecca, pointing at the phone wildly with one of his fingers. *This is it*, he mouthed silently.

Rebecca jumped from her seat. She thought she would whoop for joy. Their gamble had paid off. She could barely stand still. She noticed that she was wringing her hands as Philip jotted some information on a pad. He repeated an address on North Central Avenue, then a phone number. "Forty-five minutes," he said at last, evidently repeating some instructions while checking the clock on the wall.

"I'll call right back," he said. "First, I'm going to check out the number you gave me."

He hung up and grinned at Rebecca. "We've found him," he said, enthusiasm creeping into his voice. "I'm sure of it."

Rebecca wanted to hug him, but she dared not in the newsroom. Philip had already pulled a phone book from the desktop and was searching through the business listings.

"He says his name is Stuart Cole, Attorney-at-Law. He gave me a phone number to his office in the EquityCorp building, but I'm going to take one out of the book, give it a ring, and see who answers."

His finger traced down a column of names. "I don't want to risk wasting time with another crank." His finger slowed, then stopped. "Here it is," he exclaimed. He checked the number the man who called himself Cole had given him. "It's different," he said, keying in the number from the book, "but he might have given me the number for an unlisted line."

He waited for the connection to be made. Suddenly his eyes lit up. "Cole?" he asked. A moment of silence followed while he listened to the response. "Good," he said. "Forty-five minutes."

He hung up and turned to Rebecca, who stood breathlessly waiting to hear what he had to say.

He breathed deeply and licked his lips. "Stuart Cole is the personal representative for the estate of the man he believes was your father. His name was Jefferson Rutherford."

Rebecca repeated the name, listening to the sound of it. Then she smiled at Philip. The mystery was solved at last. After years of wondering and guessing, she finally knew her father's name.

Philip watched as she again spoke the name to herself, a curious look on his face. "You don't know who Jefferson Rutherford was, do you?" he asked.

She smiled. "He was my father," she said, explaining something that was obviously quite evident.

Philip laughed out loud and slowly seated himself. "Becky," he said, "Jefferson Rutherford was one of the richest men in the state of Arizona."

Chapter Ten

The headquarters of EquityCorp towered over the other structures on North Central Avenue. The building, bright chrome and glass by day, was dark and gray at night. A few windows shone white against the shadowy background, and the firm name glowed in blue letters along the walls of the top two stories.

Philip parked in an adjoining garage, and he and Rebecca approached the front entrance to the building. Unlike the rest of the structure, the lobby was brightly lit. Through the panels of glass, a security guard could be seen manning his station. A row of revolving doors provided access to the building. They approached the third set of doors as Cole had instructed, and Philip rapped on the glass with his keys.

They rode the elevator to the fifteenth floor, where Cole's firm had a suite of offices. Cole himself occupied an enormous corner office, expensively decorated with comfortable green-leather furniture. Windows on adjoining walls gave a panoramic view. City lights twinkled like jewels, and a full moon hovered high in the sky.

"Please have a seat," Stuart Cole said after introductions were made. He motioned to a pair of chairs arranged side by side before his enormous walnut desk. He was a heavyset man in his late sixties, with neatly groomed, graying hair. He sat in a tan, high-backed executive's chair behind the desk and surveyed the pair. The top of his desk, Rebecca noticed, was free of clutter and shone like a mirror.

"We've been waiting a long time to meet you," he said to Rebecca.

"We?" Rebecca asked.

He nodded. "I'm speaking for everyone included in the settlement of Jefferson Rutherford's estate." His voice was deep and commanding, his words spoken with deliberate speed.

Rebecca had so many questions that she didn't know where to begin. Cole didn't give her a chance to ask.

"It is important to remember," he said, "that as of this moment we have no proof that you are indeed Mr. Rutherford's daughter. The story I saw this evening on the news leads me to believe that you were, however, the object of Delbert Tipton's search." He eyed her speculatively. "I would like to ask you some questions to clarify a few points, if I may."

"I think the story pretty much said it all," Philip said.

Cole smiled at him patiently. "I'll be the judge of that."

Rebecca again detailed the events leading up to her discovery of Tipton's body in the motel room. Cole noted her answers on a yellow legal pad. When she was finished, he asked about Pepper and again jotted her responses.

Finally he laid his pencil across the pad. His gaze traveled from Rebecca to Philip, and then back to Rebecca again. "So you and your principal, Mr. Foster, found Tipton's body?"

"That's right."

"And you were on the scene with Mr. Grant when Pepper's car was recovered from the canal?"

Rebecca nodded.

Cole steepled his fingers before his face. "I've never heard of Pepper, but I knew Delbert Tipton. I hired him seven months ago to locate you." He gazed through his fingers at Rebecca. "As Mr. Rutherford's longtime attorney, I was aware that he had fathered a daughter." He paused. His eyes seemed to bore directly through Rebecca.

"Mr. Rutherford was a very wealthy man who was given to certain . . . indiscretions." He cleared his throat. "Twenty-three years ago Mr. Rutherford revealed to me that he was being threatened with a paternity suit by a woman whose name he refused to divulge. He was fifty-two years old at the time, and though his name was not yet a household word in Arizona, he owned considerable real estate up North.

"There was no doubt in his mind that the child was his, but he had no intention of marrying the woman, claiming that she meant nothing to him. Further, he didn't want to risk a scandal that might jeopardize business dealings he was about to undertake."

Cole stopped briefly to gauge the reaction of his audience. Rebecca sat tensely on the edge of her seat. "I could see no point in allowing the case to progress to court with its potential of financial ruin for my client. It seemed obvious to me, from the amount the woman was demanding as recompense, that we were dealing with a relatively unsophisticated young woman who had no idea about Mr. Rutherford's true worth. Had she hired a lawyer, however, the situation could have been drastically altered.''

Cole scanned Rebecca's face. Her deliberately impassive expression gave no clue to her feelings. ''On my advice Mr. Rutherford made a cash settlement with the woman, in exchange for a signed contract disavowing any further claims to Rutherford's assets. Because he did not want me to know the woman's name, he never showed me the signed contract, but Mr. Rutherford assured me that it did, in fact, exist.'' He cleared his throat again. ''That should have been the end of the situation.''

''It wasn't?'' Rebecca asked.

''It wasn't,'' Cole responded. ''One month later Mr. Rutherford again approached me regarding this matter. He had evidently been following the situation, and he said that the baby had been born, that it was a girl, and that the mother had given it up for adoption.'' Here the lawyer began to look slightly uncomfortable. ''He asked me if it would be possible to sue the woman for the money he had paid her. He asserted that he had made the payment on the assumption that the woman would raise the child herself. Since she had reneged on her portion of the deal, Mr. Rutherford wanted his money returned.''

''How much was it?'' Philip asked. Like Rebecca, he, too, was leaning forward on the edge of his seat.

''Ten thousand dollars,'' Cole answered.

''That's all?'' Philip questioned, incredulous.

''It was worth substantially more twenty-three years

ago,'' Cole intoned. ''In any event, it wasn't worth a lawsuit, and I advised Mr. Rutherford to simply drop the matter.''

Rebecca took a deep breath. The facts surrounding her birth had not affected her as deeply as she had once believed they might. Long ago she had accepted the fact that her arrival into this world hadn't been greeted with banners and parties. Still, she hadn't expected so tawdry a story.

''Mr. Rutherford left a clause in his will that provided for his daughter,'' Cole continued. He glanced at Rebecca. ''Aside from you, he never fathered any children, nor was he ever wed. It became increasingly important to him, as he grew older, that he make some restitution for what he came to call the greatest mistake of his life—allowing you to be adopted.''

A cough rumbled deep in his throat. Though he was clearly attempting an impartial tone, it was obvious that he was uncomfortable relating Rebecca's earliest days as though she had been a stock option.

''He dared not make this restitution during his lifetime, however,'' Cole continued, ''for fear of possible lawsuits. Instead, he rewrote his will, including a proviso that, upon his death, his estate not be divided until an investigation had been made to locate his daughter. Further, because he feared that a lengthy probate would substantially jeopardize his holdings, he stipulated that the investigation should last for no longer than exactly seven months after his death. Finally, he stipulated that if his daughter should be located before the expiration of that seven months and her identity subsequently proved, she should inherit under the terms of the will.''

He leaned forward and quickly summed up the provisions of the will. ''It's a bit sticky, you see. Under the will, the estate could be divided in one of two ways. If you were found, you would be included, and a certain division would be made. If, on the other hand, seven months had elapsed without your being discovered, the estate would be divided according to quite different terms.''

Rebecca sat silently for several moments, trying to comprehend everything that was being said. ''So because Tipton found me, I will be inheriting under the will.''

''Exactly.''

''And because she's inheriting,'' Philip interjected, ''I suppose that it's safe to assume someone else will be receiving a smaller portion.''

''It's a safe assumption to make,'' Cole said. ''Mr. Rutherford assigned me personal representative for his estate. It was my duty to ensure that all conditions of the will were met. Delbert Tipton ran his own highly efficient agency in Tucson. As an attorney, I often used his services. I paid his regular rate and promised him a substantial finder's fee should he locate you.

''Researching adoptions is difficult work,'' Cole continued. ''Still and all, I had expected greater progress from Tipton. I had the feeling that he was simply sitting on the case and accepting my weekly payments. Finally, just as the seven-month time limit was about to expire, he informed me that he had a lead. He said that he would be traveling to California and that if everything went according to plan, he would be bringing Mr. Rutherford's daughter back with him.

"Unfortunately, that was the last I heard of him. He would not reveal your name before his departure. Despite our previous dealings, you see, Tipton always had one eye open for the double cross. He was afraid that if I learned your identity before he brought you in, I could somehow circumvent our deal and leave him without his fee.

"Had it not been for your broadcast tonight," he concluded, "I am certain that the deadline would have passed, and you would have lost the right to inherit."

"You had no idea that Tipton had been murdered?" Philip asked.

Cole shook his head. "None at all. I expect that the authorities would have been in contact with us shortly, but interstate police cooperation isn't all that it should be. In any event," he concluded, "I've seen firsthand Tipton's brand of filing. It may have stymied the police in their attempts to draw up a client list." He smiled faintly. "Let's just say that it was designed to ensure confidentiality."

"And you didn't know Pepper?" Rebecca asked.

"I've never heard of the man. From what you tell me, it hardly seems likely that he would have been working for me, does it? There are two other heirs. It is reasonable to expect that he was working for one or both of them."

He glanced from Rebecca to Philip. "After we first spoke, I called the police," he said. "I've explained my connection with Tipton and how the Rutherford estate figures prominently in the deaths of both the murdered investigators. I'm certain that they'll want to speak with you.'' He allowed a shadow of a smile. ''Especially after your barbed comment on the news.''

He abruptly switched his train of thought. ''Mr. Rutherford was a financial genius,'' he said. ''His holdings in real estate, hospitality, and communications systems made him one of the richest men in Arizona. He was also temperamental, moody, and almost impossible to work for. A moment of brilliance could be followed in the next instant by a childish outburst. You will have to judge for yourself what type of man your father was.''

He searched Rebecca's face for a clue to her thoughts but found nothing. ''Meanwhile, I think we should meet the others named in Mr. Rutherford's will.''

''They're here?'' Philip asked.

Cole gestured toward a door on the side wall. ''As a matter of fact, they've been waiting for you in the other room.''

Rebecca glanced anxiously at Philip. ''One of them is the killer,'' she said.

Philip's eyes narrowed. He turned to Cole. ''Whoever killed Tipton and Pepper didn't want Rebecca located,'' he said. ''I don't think it would be wise, or safe, to bring her in.''

Cole nodded thoughtfully. ''It is,'' he began, speaking with deliberate care, ''entirely possible, probable even, that parties responsible for the deaths of both Mr. Tipton and Mr. Pepper are somehow connected with Mr. Rutherford's will.'' He nodded at her reassuringly. ''But you are hardly entering a den of snarling jackals. Further, inasmuch as your last-minute showing significantly affects the division of the estate, introducing yourself is simply a matter of common courtesy.''

He splayed his hands flat across his desk. ''In any event, the deadline for your appearance is rapidly approaching.'' He eyed his watch significantly. ''We could delay the meeting until tomorrow morning, but that might lead to future legal trouble. It is possible that suit could be filed to block your inheritance because you did not present yourself to the other heirs. The wording in the will is a bit vague in this area, and it would be a cruel irony if, after all this, you were to lose your inheritance on a technicality.''

Rebecca breathed deeply. ''You'll be all right,'' Philip said. ''The killer was trying to prevent you from meeting the deadline. Now that you've made it, you're safe.'' He smiled reassurance at her.

''It's true, Ms. Brown,'' Cole said, evidently noting her perplexed expression. ''No one stands to profit by your death. The murders of Pepper and Tipton will be investigated, and I assure you that with the narrow pool of suspects, an arrest will be made shortly.''

''It seems I don't have much choice,'' Rebecca said.

Cole nodded. ''I'm afraid that you're entirely correct. But before we go to meet them, let me tell you about the other heirs: Jefferson Rutherford's younger brother, Benjamin, and his nephew, Benjamin's son, Wendell.''

Rebecca listened to their names silently, certain that one of them was a murderer.

The attorney continued, ''Benjamin Rutherford is sixty-nine years old. He has been a partner in his brother's ventures since the beginning. Originally Benjamin was to have inherited a considerably larger share of Jefferson's estate, but two years ago, when Benjamin divorced his wife of forty-four years and married a woman young enough to be his daughter, Jefferson redistributed the estate. Mind you, he had little use for sympathy, and he did not change the will because he was unhappy with Benjamin's domestic affairs. Rather, he was certain that Benjamin's new wife, Monique, was a gold digger intent on plundering the Rutherford wealth."

"A real sentimentalist," Philip snorted.

"I was not retained by Mr. Rutherford to judge his actions," Cole responded. "I simply handle his affairs. Now, as for nephew Wendell," he continued, "Benjamin's son." He paused for a moment. "He was born shortly before you," he told Rebecca. "Coming late, as he did, in Benjamin's life, he was severely spoiled. Jefferson had little use for him but left him a substantial share of his estate simply because he represented the only heir capable of sustaining the Rutherford name."

Cole shook his head. "He showed up tonight, drunk, as usual, carting along this week's girlfriend." He paused while he appeared to search his memory. "Sammi," he said, making no effort to mask his distaste. "Sammi Stewart. An obnoxious little girl with a very big mouth." He shook his head, then added dryly, "A true intellectual. She describes herself as a poet and an artist."

"They're waiting for us in the other room?" Rebecca asked.

Cole smiled thinly. "This may be a bit unpleasant. You see, both Benjamin and Wendell were, naturally, at the original reading of the will. Benjamin was to have received seventy percent, and Wendell the remainder. They also knew what would happen if you should happen to be found.'' He paused.

''And what *would* happen?'' Philip asked.

Cole fixed his eyes on Rebecca. ''Benjamin would receive controlling interest of fifty-one percent in all commercial holdings and investments. And you, Ms. Brown,'' he said slowly, ''would receive everything else.''

Rebecca sat speechless, dumbfounded.

''What does that amount to in dollars?'' she heard Philip ask.

''Somewhere in the tens of millions,'' Cole replied.

She turned to look at Philip. ''It's impossible,'' she said.

Philip grinned. ''You can plan on buying your own dinners from now on.''

Rebecca felt as though she were in a daze. Tens of millions of dollars. The figure was so enormous that it was incomprehensible.

Cole cleared his throat. ''Wendell, of course, has also been provided for.'' Rebecca thought she saw genuine humor shine momentarily in his eyes.

''Now,'' he said, rising from his chair, ''I believe we have some business to take care of before we begin buying dinners.'' He circled the desk. ''This way.'' He crossed to the connecting door.

They entered the adjoining office. It had been artfully decorated to resemble an expensively appointed family room. A splash of contemporary Southwestern colors blended well with an extensive collection of Danish modern furniture. A wide-screen television and sound system were recessed into one wall, and a large, round fireplace was tucked neatly into a corner. In another corner was a fully stocked wet bar. Large, green-leafed potted plants were scattered here and there.

Nothing belied the fact that the room adjoined the law office of Stuart Cole. Business, obviously, was good.

Four faces turned to greet them as they entered, and the sound of low conversation abruptly ceased.

Rebecca and Philip followed Cole into the room. Several pieces of furniture had been arranged around a large, expensive-looking Navajo rug in the center of the floor.

He motioned to a pair of chairs, and they sat down.

Philip seemed completely at ease, settling into his seat and crossing his leg over his knee. Rebecca felt as though she were under the lens of a microscope. She returned the stares of the four in the room silently.

An older man, obviously Benjamin, eyed her impassively. He was seated on a sofa almost directly across from her. He wore a conservative blue suit and a red tie. He looked every inch the conservative businessman, except for the platinum blonde clinging to his arm.

Rebecca quickly sized up Monique Rutherford. A youngish-looking thirty, she wore a wedding band as wide as a belt. The diamond on her engagement ring could have financed a fleet of limousines. Her gold lamé evening gown was slit almost to the hip, and she was twisted at just the right angle to expose a long, shapely leg.

Jefferson Rutherford had been right about her, Rebecca thought. Monique inhaled lightly on a long cigarette and returned her gaze.

To the side, in a pair of chairs identical to the ones in which she and Philip sat, were two others. Wendell Rutherford wore a pair of blue jeans and a polo shirt open at the collar. His blond hair was long but combed stylishly. His face was twisted in contempt. In his hands he held a half-empty highball glass.

The girl, Sammi, looked barely old enough to be out of high school, though she had obviously matured quickly. She was wearing a black miniskirt, black tights, and a black turtleneck sweater. Her hair was cropped short and was dyed, of course, black. A layer of pancake gave her a startlingly white face from which blazed a pair of ruby red lips. On her arms were dozens of bracelets of all colors and shapes. "Charmed," she said arrogantly when Rebecca's eyes met hers.

Cole stood in the center of the carpet. "As I told you all when I called earlier this evening," he began, allowing his gaze to shift from the older man with the young wife to the younger man with the highball, "I had some rather significant information regarding Jefferson Rutherford's will." He paused dramatically. "I believe that we have located Mr. Rutherford's daughter." He glanced toward Rebecca. "May I introduce Ms. Rebecca Brown."

"It's a lie!" Wendell shouted, exploding to his feet. He pointed at Cole. "You're trying to rip me off."

Rebecca jerked back with surprise at the unexpected uproar. She glanced quickly toward Philip. His eyes were narrowed, locked on the shouting man.

"I'll get a lawyer," Wendell shouted. "You're not going to do this to me."

Cole stood silently, his unassuming control of the situation unscathed by the outburst. "Sit down, Wen-*dell*," he commanded. The lilt in his voice gave Rebecca the impression that he was enjoying the entire scene.

"I'll sit down when I want to," Wendell retorted. He stalked across the room to the bar, moving with the exaggerated care of someone who has had too much to drink.

"Don't you think you've had enough?" Cole asked, noting his condition.

"Yeah, I've had enough," Wendell slurred. "Enough of you." He spilled a shot of bourbon into his glass.

Cole turned his attention to the older man. "With Ms. Brown is Philip Grant," he said, continuing the introductions as though the interruption had never occurred. "You may recognize Mr. Grant as a reporter with Channel 6 news."

Philip nodded a silent greeting.

Benjamin Rutherford rose from the sofa and introduced himself, extending his hand to both Philip and Rebecca. He then introduced Monique, who smiled acknowledgement over the cigarette she held nimbly between her fingers.

Wendell half-lurched, half-sauntered back to his seat. "You're not going to get away with this," he muttered, extending a drink to his girlfriend. "That's my money."

"And you can't extort it," Sammi said.

Wendell sneered. "Me and Sammi have plans for that money."

"We're going to open our own gallery," she informed them, sipping her drink. She flashed Rebecca a look of sublime boredom. "And you're not invited."

''That's right—they're not invited,'' Wendell said, tilting back and forth like a flagpole in a breeze. He turned toward Rebecca, sloshing his drink in the process. ''You're not getting anything of mine, not even a Christmas card.''

Cole eyed the pair with a look of distaste. ''As you know,'' he said, ''Jefferson Rutherford's will stipulated that should his daughter be found within seven months of his passing, his entire estate would be divided between the daughter and his brother, with Benjamin receiving a controlling interest.''

He turned to Rebecca. ''I believe that Rebecca Brown *is* Jefferson Rutherford's daughter. I further note that the time is 11:35 P.M., which means that Ms. Brown has presented herself to me before the end of the seven-month period stipulated by Mr. Rutherford, which was to end at midnight tonight.''

Wendell pointed a shaky finger at Cole. ''You haven't proved it,'' he shouted. ''You haven't proved that she's his daughter.''

''The will makes no provision for proof before the deadline,'' Cole stated. ''It simply requires that Rutherford's daughter show herself before midnight at the end of the seventh month after his death. Doing so makes her eligible to inherit under the will, subject, of course, to subsequent proof of kinship.''

Rebecca could see the pleasure Cole was taking from dealing with Wendell.

''She hasn't proved it,'' Wendell shouted again, oblivious to Cole's words.

''I want to see the paperwork,'' Sammi chimed in.

The lawyer continued. "I personally believe that Ms. Brown *is* Mr. Rutherford's daughter. I further believe that an examination of Delbert Tipton's records, as well as the records of relevant adoption agencies, whom I will petition in the morning, will substantiate this fact.

"As personal representative for Mr. Rutherford's estate, therefore, I am bound to declare that the seventy-thirty split of his assets, which would have gone into effect at midnight tonight, is now null and void."

"No, it isn't," Wendell shouted.

"You can't do this!" Sammi screamed, leaping to her feet beside her boyfriend.

Philip was poised on the edge of his seat, ready for anything that might occur. Rebecca waited tensely for the inevitable explosion.

"Mr. Rutherford's estate will be divided according to the terms directed in his will," Cole continued. "Fifty-one percent to Benjamin Rutherford, and forty-nine percent to Ms. Brown."

He turned to Wendell, who stood listening silently to the verdict, his face contorted in drunken rage. "And you, Wendell, will receive, according to your uncle's wishes, one dollar, that you might invest it wisely and reap the rewards."

"I'm going to sue you!" he shouted, leaping across the floor at Cole.

Philip jumped from his seat.

Wendell grabbed Cole by his necktie. "I'll squeeze this tie until your head pops off!" he screamed. Cole struggled futilely against the younger man's strength.

Philip threw a quick jab at Wendell's face, followed

by a cross to the jaw that landed the raving man on the floor.

Sammi rushed to the aid of her fallen hero, screaming at Philip. ''That's it, dude, that's it,'' she wailed. ''That's assault and battery. That's alleged premeditation.''

Cole motioned toward the adjoining door. ''I'll be with you in a minute,'' he said.

Rebecca could barely wait to escape the insane melee, but Philip seemed to back away only grudgingly. She could see the gleam in his eyes, the lust for the fight. He looked hard and mean. She was glad that he was on her side. He backed slowly across the floor.

Sammi was still screaming, waving her finger wildly at him. ''I'll see you in court.''

Philip grabbed Rebecca around the waist. ''Let's get out of here,'' he said.

Benjamin and his wife sat silently on the sofa. Monique smiled faintly, listening to Sammi's inane ravings.

''I know the law,'' she shrieked. ''You're going to jail.''

Breathing a sigh of relief, Rebecca ducked back into the sedate surroundings of Cole's private office, with Philip close behind.

Chapter Eleven

Piano music floated lightly through the elegant ambience of the Purple Room.

"It's gorgeous," Rebecca exclaimed, admiring the extravagant interior.

"I hope you don't think I'm trying to impress you," Philip said. "Because from now on you're paying for everything."

Rebecca laughed. "My pleasure."

They were seated at an intimate table in a darkened corner of the exclusive nightclub.

Soft candlelight filtered gently through the globe of red glass in which it was ensconced, casting a soft ring on the table. A grand piano on a circular stage played for silhouettes undulating gently on the dance floor.

Rebecca watched Philip's face in the mellow light, the shadows playing tricks with his eyes. He caught her staring, and she smiled shyly.

"It's unbelievable," she said. So much had happened in the past week. Only now, in the calm of the Purple Room, was reality beginning to sink in.

Philip sipped from a glass of gin and tonic. "Believe it. It's only the beginning. As soon as your identity is verified, you'll be dealing with some very big money."

Rebecca shook her head. ‘‘I never dreamed that I would have to worry about having too *much* money.’’

‘‘It’s a problem most people never have to worry about,’’ he answered lightly.

‘‘I wonder if it’s really such a joke. Look at Jefferson Rutherford. He never ruled his money; his money ruled him. The fear of losing his fortune ran his life.’’ She paused for a moment, then said firmly, ‘‘I’ll never let that happen to me.’’

‘‘If you ever forget, I’ll be sure to remind you.’’

‘‘I’m sure you will,’’ she said with a smile. Her thoughts returned to Rutherford. ‘‘He died a rich man, but really he had nothing. No family, no close friends. The only thing that kept Wendell around was his hope for an inheritance.’’

Philip nodded. ‘‘In the end, he gave almost half of everything he’d ever owned to a daughter he’d never seen. One he wasn’t even sure could be found.’’ After a short pause he added, ‘‘I don’t think the police will have much work finding out who killed Tipton and Pepper. I’d be surprised if Wendell isn’t behind bars before tomorrow noon.’’

‘‘He was definitely spooky,’’ Rebecca agreed. ‘‘And that weird girlfriend of his. . . .’’ She shook her head.

Philip smiled. ‘‘She really had me worried about that ‘alleged premeditation.’ ’’

‘‘Don’t you wonder how people like that always seem to meet each other?’’

‘‘So much for the theory that opposites attract,’’ Philip said. He glanced absently around the lounge. ‘‘I suppose that Wendell decided to kill Tipton when he realized that you had been found and that his fortune was in jeopardy."

"But how would he have known where to find him?"

"He followed him," Philip said. "Just like Pepper. Tipton's job was no secret, after all. He was hired by Cole specifically to meet the conditions of the will."

"Pepper," Rebecca said, remembering. "We still don't know who hired him or why he was killed."

"It will all come out as soon as Wendell is booked and printed. I have a feeling that the threat of life behind bars could generate a lot of cooperation from someone like Wendell."

"What do you mean someone like Wendell?"

Philip shrugged. "Spoiled, arrogant, and soft. He's never worked for anything in his life. You can bet that he'll wiggle, turn, and crawl on his knees and beg if he thinks it might cut one day off the time he's going to do. But he will do some time, at least. He'll pay the price for his greed."

"I wonder what comes first," Rebecca mused, "the money or the greed."

"The more you have, the more you want. Money and greed go hand in hand. And, speaking of things that go hand in hand, would you care to dance?"

Rebecca glanced toward the floor. Couples were vague, intertwined shapes in the subdued lighting. She sipped her wine. A couple returning from a dance sat at a nearby table. The woman was wearing a black gown with a plunging neckline.

"I think I'm a little underdressed," Rebecca said.

Philip followed her eyes, then gave her an appraising gaze. "A little overdressed is more like it."

She arched her eyebrows.

Philip leaned forward. "You obviously don't know how the world works, so I'm going to give you a little lesson."

He leaned back in his seat and sipped his drink. "If Rebecca Brown, honest, hardworking teacher, tried to get into the Purple Room wearing cutoffs and a tube top, she'd be put out on the street. But if Rebecca Brown, heir to the Rutherford fortune, showed up in the same get-up, she'd set off a new fashion craze."

Rebecca smiled. "Are you suggesting that I go home and cut off a pair of jeans?" she asked.

"I'm suggesting that you're beautiful no matter what you wear," he said. Then he grinned. "But I must admit we're lucky that the dress code is relaxed here during the summer, or we'd never have been allowed in."

"I told you that you should have let me change before the interview," Rebecca reminded him.

"Next time we come, you can wear a five-hundred-dollar gown and be the envy of everyone," he said. "But tonight you're going to dance."

He rose from his seat and gripped her wrist lightly, tugging it gently. Rebecca relented with a smile, and he guided her onto the floor.

Soft piano chords fluttered gently in the shadows. He placed his hands on her waist, then circled them slowly around to the small of her back before drawing her near to him.

Magic surrounded her like a velvet cocoon. She leaned

into Philip's chest; the music sparkled like starlight in a dark sky.

She held him tightly, savoring his strength, thrilling at the muscles that crisscrossed his back. Slowly they undulated from side to side, his warm breath in her ear.

She surrendered herself to him, burying her cheek in his chest. His lips traced slowly along the line of her jaw, and she tilted her face to his for a long, slow kiss.

"I love you," he whispered in her ear, so quietly that even the delicate notes of the piano nearly covered his words.

Rebecca's heart swelled with joy. Gone were the fears of heartbreak that had for so long ruled her life. "I love you too," she responded. Simply speaking the words filled her with happiness.

Philip pulled her tightly to him. She leaned into his body, and they sealed their vows with another unending, rapturous kiss.

They danced until the music stopped, or maybe longer. So lost was Rebecca in her ecstasy that time itself ceased to exist.

Finally the dance floor was clear, and they had no choice but to return to their seats.

"I think we should be going," he said, glancing at his watch. "I have to get to work in the morning."

She watched him, doubting if work was really on his mind.

"Does that look you're giving me mean that you want another dance?" he asked.

She smiled. "No, I'm just wondering where I'll stay tonight."

"With me, of course," he responded, as though nothing in the world could have been more obvious. "Remember? You moved in."

"I didn't exactly move in. And I'm not sure that staying with you now would be such a good idea."

"I think it's a great idea."

"That's what I mean," she countered.

A hurt look crossed his face. "Don't forget the reason you decided to stay with me in the first place," he reminded her. "Whoever killed Tipton and Pepper is still on the prowl."

"I thought you were sure that Wendell would be in jail by tomorrow at noon," she reminded him.

"That won't do you any good tonight."

She couldn't help but smile. "It sounds as though you're actually glad a killer is out running loose."

He maintained a steady expression. "Only for tonight," he said, then smiled sheepishly. "In any event," he continued, rising from his seat, "your things are at my house, so you don't have a choice. We have to go there." He offered her his hand. "We can decide what to do about you after we get there."

"Now you make me sound like I'm a problem," she said, taking his hand.

"You're the kind of problem everyone would like to have," he responded, leading her toward the door. "Like too much money."

They crossed the parking lot, hand in hand. Suddenly a thought occurred to Rebecca. "My car," she said. "It's still parked in front of your station."

Philip opened her door. "It's safe."

"But am I?" Rebecca asked.

His arms were once again around her. "It depends on what you mean by safe," he muttered. He leaned forward to kiss her.

The boom of a gunshot split the quiet of the parking lot. Philip's head snapped to the side, and he tumbled backward onto the pavement.

"Philip!" Rebecca screamed, dropping to her knees beside him.

His hand clutched the side of his head, over his ear. "I'm all right," he said. Then, noticing that Rebecca was still exposed over the hood of his car, he grabbed her by the wrist and pulled. "Get down," he commanded.

Another gunshot exploded as she fell forward. She covered her head in fear, prone on the warm blacktop.

A car engine raced on the street. Philip scrambled to his knees and peered over the hood of his car.

The squeal of spinning tires met Rebecca's ears. The car accelerated down the street, the sound of its engine diminishing with distance.

"He's gone," Philip said. "A white Porsche." He wiped his hand across the side of his head, then checked the blood that smeared his palm. "Are you all right?" he asked.

She climbed to her feet, trying bravely to fight back the tears that threatened to burst forth at any moment. "I'm fine," she said, "but you. . . ." Her heart was pounding with fear.

"I'm okay," he said. "Just grazed." He glanced again at his bloody palm. "Even small head wounds seem to bleed forever," he added, trying to soothe her fears.

He stood beside her, one hand around her shoulders, the other pressed to his head, attempting to stem the flow of blood.

"I thought it was all over," she said.

She heard footsteps pounding on the pavement, and confused cries of, "What's happening, what's happening?"

Suddenly she burst into tears of fear and helplessness. Philip tightened his hold on her. "Call the police," he shouted. "There's been a shooting."

Chapter Twelve

The detectives' bullpen at the Phoenix police department was almost a carbon copy of the LAPD squad room where Rebecca had, only one week earlier, given a statement detailing her involvement in Tipton's murder.

The room was crowded with the same beige office furniture. Desks were arranged in pairs, butted head to head against each other, and stacks of documents and manila file folders were scattered across their tops. Along the walls, rows of filing cabinets contained the paperwork the desks couldn't hold.

Sergeant Holmstead, a middle-aged detective with a graying mustache and the beginning of a paunch, scribbled on an official form as Rebecca answered his questions.

"Would either of you care for coffee?" he asked, interrupting the questioning briefly.

"I could use some," Philip answered.

Rebecca shook her head. The last thing she needed was something to help keep her awake. She wished that she could lie down, close her eyes, and sleep for a week.

Holmstead shook his head to clear the cobwebs. "These mid shifts kill me," he said. "We have a four-month rotation. Four months working days, then four eves, and four mids. Eves don't bother me, but mids are killers.''

He shook his head again. ''Coffee,'' he said, waving an index finger, as though he'd just remembered. ''Back in a minute.'' He glanced at Philip. ''Cream? Sugar?''

''Black.''

They watched Holmstead's back as he retreated to a far corner of the squad room for the coffee. He began a conversation there with a uniformed officer.

Rebecca glanced at the clock on the wall. It was nearing two-thirty. She looked back at Philip. A thick white bandage jutted from the side of his head, secured by long lengths of hospital tape to what the nurses had left of his hair.

She felt tears again coming to her eyes. ''I'm so sorry,'' she said.

Philip prodded the bandage gently with his fingers. ''It's not so bad,'' he assured her. ''For now at least, the bandage is covering the haircut.''

She had no idea how he maintained his sense of humor, but she was thankful that he did. ''You could have been killed,'' she said.

''I guess we're both lucky that I have a hard head.''

''I'm not joking,'' she insisted. ''If anything had happened, it would have been my fault.''

He let his rolling eyes express his dismay. ''In any event,'' he said when he'd finished the pantomime, ''I wouldn't be so sure that nothing *has* happened. When Blanchard learns that we were out celebrating until the wee hours, *he'll* kill me.''

Rebecca recalled Philip's stricken look when the blue-and-white Channel 6 news van had pulled up in front of the Purple Room and a reporter had jumped out with Jay the cameraman at his side. "Phil?" he'd asked with an I-can't-believe-it's-you tone.

"You don't think he'll fire you, do you?" Rebecca asked.

"Blanchard plays it strictly by the book. I told him there was nothing between us. Now he'll know there was. Doing personal favors for friends at company expense isn't the best way to curry favor with the boss."

"Maybe you should have just told him the truth from the beginning," Rebecca offered.

"Gee," he responded sarcastically, "you have a true gift for insight."

"There's no need to get mad at me for it," she snapped. "Trouble at work seems pretty small compared to the fact that you were almost murdered. Anyway, you got a pretty good story, even if it did come to you through a friend, and it looks like it's only going to get bigger."

"I'm sorry," Philip said. "I'm just getting tired." He tapped the bandage again. "My head's starting to ache, and don't forget," he added good-naturedly, "someone woke me bright and early this morning."

"You told me you were already awake," Rebecca said with a grin. She watched Philip, who continued to poke at the bandage. He winced and jerked his hand away. "You should leave it alone," she scolded.

"Thanks, Mom," he retorted. "Maybe you could kiss it and make it better."

"Not if you ask me in that tone of voice."

Holmstead returned with two cups of coffee and a cellophane-wrapped package of miniature donuts. ''I hope you like toasted coconut,'' he said, peeling off the wrapper and helping himself to one. He set the remainder on his desk. Philip immediately reached for one and dunked it into his coffee.

''I caught your bit on the news tonight,'' he told Philip.

''That right?''

''Sure,'' Holmstead said. ''I watch the news every night before beginning my shift.''

Philip sipped his coffee.

''It's a shame about the police,'' Holmstead continued ''Not helping you and all.''

''It's just a matter of keeping potential victims informed,'' Philip said.

Holmstead shrugged. ''It's more a matter of police procedure. Believe it or not, we get the job done all by ourselves occasionally.''

''This one shouldn't be too tough,'' Philip said.

Holmstead read his report silently. ''You suspect this Wendell Rutherford of firing the shots at you in the parking lot tonight?''

''I can just about guarantee it.''

Holmstead raised his eyebrows. ''That's why you should leave the police work to the professionals.''

''What do you mean by that?''

''It's funny the things you hear by the coffee machine on the mid shift,'' Holmstead said. ''For instance, we put out an APB on that white Porsche you saw speeding away from the scene. A patrol car is bringing in the shooter. Should be here any minute.''

Rebecca sat forward. ‘‘They caught Wendell?’’ she asked.

‘‘Nope. Wendell wasn’t even in the car. According to the arresting officer’s radio report, her name is Sammi Stewart.’’

Rebecca was floored. ‘‘Sammi? A killer?’’

‘‘Had a .38 on the seat beside her. Told the arresting officer that she pulled the trigger.’’ Holmstead pretended to read the reports. ‘‘You mentioned something about a .38 being used to kill both Tipton and Pepper, didn’t you?’’ he asked.

Without waiting for an answer, he continued. ‘‘We dug a .38 slug from the wood trim on the eaves of the Purple Room. The lab’s running a test on it right now to see if it matches the one we took out of Pepper.’’

He rubbed the side of his nose with an index finger and smiled at Philip. ‘‘And we did it all without your help,’’ he said. ‘‘I wonder whether we’ll ever see that on the news at ten.’’

‘‘I think you probably will,’’ Philip told him, sitting back in his seat.

‘‘Glad to hear it. Now let’s get these reports finished up.’’ Holmstead turned to the documents and resumed his questions regarding the night’s events.

The lights were on in Philip’s living room. Rebecca and Philip were discussing the night’s events, unable to sleep. Suddenly someone rang the doorbell.

‘‘Who could that be?’’ Rebecca asked, looking at the clock.

‘‘At four in the morning,’’ Philip responded, ‘‘I doubt

if it's anyone we want to see.'' A shadowy form could be seen on the porch through the pebbled glass.

He crossed to the front door and peered through the peephole. ''It's Wendell,'' he said, sounding surprised.

''I can see you in there,'' Wendell whined loudly. ''I know you're home. Open up.''

Philip looked questioningly at Rebecca. She shook her head no.

''Come on,'' Wendell wailed. ''Please. I have to talk to someone.''

Philip continued to spy on him through the peephole. ''I think he's crying.''

''Find out what he wants,'' Rebecca said.

Philip called the question through the door.

''I just want to talk,'' Wendell pleaded. By the tone of his voice, it was now obvious that he was in tears. ''Sammi didn't kill anyone. She wouldn't hurt a fly.''

''She took a shot at us,'' Philip said.

''She's my beautiful little angel,'' Wendell sobbed. ''And now she's in prison. How can an angel go to jail? How?''

Philip shook his head. ''I'm not going to let him stand out there and cry all night long. He'll wake up the entire complex.''

''Philip,'' Rebecca reminded him angrily, ''until just an hour ago we thought he was a murderer. We still can't be sure he isn't.''

''This guy isn't going to hurt anyone,'' he answered. He faced the door. ''All right,'' he called. ''I'm going to open the door, but I'm going to search you before you come in.''

''She's my little baby angel,'' Wendell blubbered.

Philip opened the door and stepped outside to frisk him before they reentered.

Wendell followed Philip into the room, hanging his head low, rubbing his tearing eyes, and dragging his feet disconsolately on the floor. He sniffed loudly. ''She never killed anyone,'' he insisted. He shuffled to a chair and plopped down. ''How could an angel kill anyone?'' He pouted quietly for several seconds.

''First things first, Wendell,'' Philip said at last. He stood over Wendell like a parent about to scold a child. ''How did you know where I lived?''

Wendell rubbed his nose and stared at his shoes. ''Pepper told us,'' he said.

''Pepper?'' Philip repeated. He shot a glance at Rebecca. ''Was he working for you?''

''Not exactly.''

Philip's hands were on his hips. ''You're either going to answer straight, Wendell, or I'm going to boot you back onto the street. Do you want everyone to see you crying?''

''I don't care if the whole world sees me,'' he said, raising his tearstained face to Philip's. ''I love my little angel. I'm not ashamed to care enough to cry.''

''Then cry someplace else,'' Philip retorted.

Wendell dropped his face and sniffed rapidly several times.

''Now,'' Philip said, ''did you hire Pepper?''

Wendell shook his head. ''Not by myself. We all did. I mean, when Uncle Jeff died and they read the will, my dad and I and Monique decided that we should hire a detective to make sure his daughter never came around for her share.''

``How long ago did you hire him?''

Wendell blinked back his tears. ``Right after Cole read the will and told us that he was going to hire Tipton. We had a secret meeting, just my dad, Monique, and me, and we decided that we would hire someone, too, someone who would watch out for our own interests.''

Satisfied that Wendell's crying was finished for the moment, Philip crossed to the sofa and sat beside Rebecca. ``You were worried about your inheritance?''

``Wouldn't you be?'' When only silence met his question, he continued. ``We were happy with the original seventy-thirty split. My dad is a businessman, but me, I don't care about it. Thirty percent was good enough.''

``And you had Pepper working on this ever since Tipton was hired.''

He nodded. ``That's right. At first my dad let him handle the investigation his own way, but later we decided to pay him simply to follow Tipton.''

``He worked for you for seven months. It must have added up to quite a bill.''

Wendell snorted. He watched them with bloodshot eyes. ``It barely put a dent in our bank accounts. If Tipton led him to my uncle's daughter, Pepper was supposed to offer her one hundred thousand dollars to keep quiet.''

``He offered fifty,'' Rebecca stated.

``That doesn't surprise me,'' Wendell said. ``He was a total rip-off. That's why my dad took him off his own investigation and put him on Tipton's trail to begin with.''

The room was silent for several seconds.

Philip spoke quietly. ‘‘What were Pepper’s instructions if Rebecca turned down his cash settlement?’’

‘‘I don’t know. Dad didn’t think it would happen. He said he’d take care of any problems.’’

Rebecca felt a chill run up her spine. She could imagine what he’d meant by that.

Suddenly Wendell’s bottom lip began to quiver, and the tears began to flow. ‘‘And now,’’ he said, ‘‘now Sammi’s in jail for something she didn’t do.’’

Philip watched him cry. ‘‘She confessed to shooting at us,’’ he pointed out.

Wendell buried his face into his clenched fists. ‘‘They’re going to charge her with murder. For killing Tipton and Pepper, and I know she didn’t do it. My angel would never hurt anyone.’’

Philip stood. ‘‘Your angel did this,’’ he said, pointing to the bandage on his head.

‘‘No, no, no!’’ Wendell shrieked. ‘‘She didn’t kill anyone. Dad did. I know he did. I can prove it.’’

‘‘What?’’ Philip asked, frozen.

‘‘Your father?’’ Rebecca said.

They waited for another burst of Wendell’s sobbing to subside. ‘‘They say that the bullets from the gun Sammi used tonight match bullets taken from the bodies of Tipton and Pepper. But I never even had that gun until tonight.’’

‘‘Take a deep breath, Wendell, and get ahold of yourself,’’ Philip commanded.

Wendell faced Philip, then Rebecca, beseeching them to believe. ‘‘Sammi couldn’t have killed them, because we didn’t have the gun. It’s my dad’s.’’

Rebecca glanced at Philip, whose face mirrored her

own doubts. ''How did Sammi end up with it in your car?'' she asked.

He sniffed loudly. ''It was all my fault. I promised Sammi that we would open a gallery for her art.'' He glanced at Rebecca. ''You remember, we told you that?'' he asked, as if it had been mentioned during a peaceful conversation at a coffee shop.

She nodded.

He swallowed and continued. ''Then Cole called and told us that Tipton had located you.'' He glanced at Rebecca again. ''Then Pepper called. First he called my dad; then he called me. He told us both the same thing He told us where Tipton was staying and said it looked like he was finally on the right trail. He said it was time for the big showdown.''

''In other words, this was where he was going to make his big play to buy off Rebecca?'' Philip asked.

Wendell nodded. ''I told Sammi about it, and she went crazy. She thought the whole world was coming to an end, I guess. I told her Pepper would take care of everything, but she, but she . . . .'' He burst into another round of tears.

''What did she do, Wendell?'' Rebecca asked.

''I don't know,'' he said. ''She ran away for a couple of days. She didn't think we were going to be able to open the gallery, so she said she was going to Flagstaff, where she had some friends who could help her. Real friends, she called them, as if I weren't her real friend.'' He wiped the tears from his cheeks.

It seemed to Rebecca that Wendell's story was only making a stronger case for the police. Sammi had obviously been using Wendell for the money he was planning to inherit, and when it appeared that his inheritance was in jeopardy, she'd decided to take matters into her own hands.

"She knew the name of the motel where Tipton was staying?" Rebecca asked.

"Yes, I told her after talking to Pepper."

"So she could have. . . ."

"I told you my angel wouldn't hurt anyone. I can prove my father did it."

"How?" Philip asked.

"Well," he began, licking his lips, "I got a call from Pepper the night she left, telling me that Tipton had been murdered in his hotel room and that he'd been killed with a .38. I own a .38 that I keep in my closet, so I went to check on it. I mean, Sammi was so freaked about everything, I was thinking that maybe, you know. . . ." The thought trailed into silence. "It was missing."

Philip nodded. "Sammi took your gun."

He nodded. "I was afraid that she might be crazy enough to go after Tipton, or"—he looked at Rebecca—"you. But I couldn't call the police, not on Sammi. You don't know her like I do. She loves everyone."

"So far, Wendell, not only have you not given us any proof that Sammi is innocent; you've just about put the rope around her neck," Philip said. "She was outraged that you might lose your inheritance, so she took your gun, and she disappeared for a couple of days." He tapped gently at the bandage on his head. "Don't forget what she did to me."

Wendell continued as though he hadn't heard. "She

showed up yesterday afternoon and said that she'd decided to stay with me.'' He smiled faintly, remembering. ''It was the happiest day of my life.''

''We need the proof, Wendell,'' Philip said.

He squinched his eyes tightly for a moment, then continued. ''We were at my house last night, and Cole called and said that according to a news broadcast he had just seen, both Tipton and Pepper had been murdered. It was the first I'd heard that Pepper was dead too.

''I checked my closet and found the gun on the shelf. I asked Sammi about it, and she told me that she'd borrowed it because she was worried about driving alone to Flagstaff. But I started thinking that maybe Sammi had done something severe.''

''Sounds like she did, Wendell.''

Wendell's eyes pleaded. ''But she didn't. Because there's something you don't know.''

He let his gaze wander from Philip to Rebecca. ''My dad is a gun collector. Uncle Jeff gave him a matched pair of .38's several years ago. I guess they were valuable or something. They had a famous name.'' He waved his arm around trying to recall the name. ''Anyway,'' he continued, ''my dad gave me one of them last year because I keep a lot of money lying around, and he thought I needed some protection from being ripped off.

''As soon as I discovered the gun on the shelf of my closet, I began to worry that maybe it had been used in two murders, and I wanted to get it out of the house.

''I drove over to my dad's. He and Monique had just taken Cole's call and were getting ready for the meeting in his office. I guess I was ranting and raving, and they didn't feel like listening, so they left me alone while they dressed. That's when I made the switch.''

''The switch?'' Rebecca asked.

''No wait, don't tell me,'' Philip interrupted. ''You took the gun your father had given you, the one that Sammi had stolen just before she disappeared. You took that gun and swapped it for its identical partner in your father's gun collection.''

Wendell couldn't meet Philip's gaze. ''That's right,'' he said. ''He keeps his guns in a big case in the rec room. He doesn't keep it locked. I walked in and put my gun in the place of his.''

Philip looked at Rebecca with disbelief; then he turned once again to Wendell. ''You're a real prize. You set your own father up to take a murder rap.''

''I didn't think Sammi really killed anybody,'' he whined in his own defense.

''Then why trade guns?'' Philip pressed.

''It doesn't matter, anyway,'' Wendell said, ''because I ended up pinning the murders on Sammi.''

Rebecca saw clearly the point he was making. ''You exchanged the gun from your closet with the gun in your father's collection, and it was your father's gun that Sammi fired at us tonight.''

''That's right,'' Wendell said, and his eyes once again brimmed with tears. ''I should have known that Sammi could never hurt anyone. But now I've messed everything up.''

''Have you gone to the police with this?'' Rebecca asked.

He laughed bitterly. "Who would believe me?" More tears welled in his eyes. "After I made the switch, I tossed my father's gun into my car, then picked up Sammi and headed for the meeting in Cole's office. Sammi wouldn't let me drive, because she said I'd been drinking. She saw the gun—it was right on top of the seat. I told her that I was carrying it because we were going to be driving through downtown.

"After the meeting Sammi told me to take a cab home." He looked at Philip. "She was mad because I let you get away with sucker punching me." He shook his head. "I guess she took my car and followed you."

He stopped for a moment. "I know she wasn't trying to hurt you when she shot at you. She was probably just trying to scare you. I mean, she was pretty tweeked about losing her gallery and everything."

He looked from Philip to Rebecca for sympathy. Receiving none, he continued. "When she shot at you, it was my father's gun she was using. The one I'd just traded for." He stared dejectedly at the floor, a single teardrop gliding over his cheek. "Now they've locked her away. How will my angel fly behind bars?" His lower lip quivered. "I was only trying to do what was best."

"Right," Philip said with a snort. "You were trying to set up your father."

Wendell was silent for a moment. "I guess he didn't need setting up, after all."

"You haven't really given us any proof," Rebecca said. "How do you expect us to believe you? You keep telling us that Sammi wouldn't hurt anyone, but she tried to kill us tonight. Not only that, but she did it with a gun that's been used in two other murders.''

''I'm telling you the truth,'' Wendell whined. He broke down again into tears. ''Who will believe me?'' he asked himself. ''Who?''

Chapter Thirteen

"The problem," Rebecca said, "is knowing whether to believe Wendell or not."

"It's not going to be an easy one to solve," Philip agreed.

They were seated side by side in a wide booth at an all-night coffee shop. An occasional car passed along the darkened street beyond the window.

Rebecca watched one cruise past and wondered where anyone could possibly be going at four-thirty in the morning.

She sipped at her coffee and leaned her head back against Philip's arm, which was resting across her shoulders. She closed her eyes. "I'm too tired to think and too wound up to sleep."

Philip adjusted his arm and said, "Just when I thought it was over, it seems it's really just beginning."

"I think Wendell is telling the truth," she said, eyes still closed. "I don't think anyone could make up a story as complicated as the one he's telling."

"That's a heck of a reason for believing him. Remember, I told you that Wendell was the kind of guy who would wiggle and squirm to get off the hook."

"He's not on the hook," she reminded him.

"But his girlfriend is. He could be lying to get her off."

"Would you lie for me?"

"I already did, remember? I still have to face Blanchard this morning." He checked his watch. "We have about four more hours to get to the bottom of this thing."

"I doubt if you'll be in any trouble," Rebecca said.

"I don't. That's why I'm trying to keep my mind on Wendell. You know, Wendell could be lying for reasons other than protecting his girlfriend. He could be the murderer."

"I don't think so."

"You were sure that he was not too long ago," Philip reminded her.

"That was before I saw how broken up he was. I don't think he was faking."

A waitress appeared carrying a coffeepot. She refilled their cups with a quick comment and a smile, pretending she didn't notice the bandage on Philip's head, then returned to a magazine she was reading at the counter.

"No one doubts that Sammi fired at us this evening," Philip said. "She's confessed to that much. But she was using Wendell's gun, and she was driving Wendell's car." He sipped his coffee. "That's a pretty strange coincidence. When you take into consideration the fact that Wendell was going to lose a fortune because of you, the coincidence starts to fade and he suddenly becomes the number-one suspect."

"I can understand why he might have killed Tipton," Rebecca agreed. "Tipton could lead me to my inheritance. But why would he kill Pepper?"

"Because Pepper knew who you were. He was the only one who could connect you to the Rutherford fortune. Even if you had agreed to accept his proposition and give up your search, Pepper would always have known where he could find you.''

''But the estate would have been settled.''

Philip glanced at her with a smile. ''As far as courts go, nothing is ever settled. Had you suddenly appeared five years from now and laid claim to the estate, I'm certain that you would have had a good chance of receiving something.''

She nodded. ''So you think that Pepper was killed because he could have become a loose cannon.''

''Probably. You heard for yourself. Pepper had been authorized to pay one hundred thousand dollars for a settlement, but he only offered you fifty. He was obviously going to pocket the other half.'' He sipped again at his coffee. ''Would you have trusted him?''

She shook her head. ''The motive seems obvious when you put it that way.''

''And let's be honest,'' he added. ''Sammi was upset tonight about losing the fortune, but all she really had riding on the deal was Wendell's promise of a gallery. I don't think she would have killed two private investigators just to protect something like that.''

''People have been killed for less.''

''That's true,'' he said thoughtfully.

A pickup truck pulled into the lot, and two men in straw cowboy hats jumped from the cab.

''What we have to do,'' Rebecca said, ''is prove somehow that either Wendell is telling the truth and Benjamin really is the killer, or that he's lying.''

"And then, we have to decide whether Wendell is lying to protect his girlfriend or himself."

"It sounds like you've already decided that he's made the entire story up."

"It's a little too convenient for my tastes," Philip answered.

The cowboys entered and seated themselves at the counter. The waitress folded her magazine and went over to serve them.

"We're not accomplishing anything sitting here," Rebecca said.

Philip stared into space for a second. "I say we confront Benjamin Rutherford with Wendell's accusation."

"He'll simply deny everything," Rebecca argued, searching her own mind for a more roundabout method of testing Wendell's story.

"You don't expect him to confess, do you?" Philip asked. He nodded slightly, planning to himself. "We'll show up on his doorstep this morning, exactly at six o'clock. We'll get him out of bed and hit him with it. His reaction will tell us more than his words."

"What makes you so sure he'll talk to you? He may slam the door in your face."

"He'll think I'm covering the story," Philip answered. "People like Benjamin Rutherford hate being quoted with a 'No comment.' It makes them look bad. He'll talk."

"Then what?"

He shrugged. "We'll take it from there."

"Hey, ain't you the guy from the news?" one of the cowboys at the counter asked.

Philip turned to them and nodded a greeting.

The cowboy snapped his fingers, trying to remember Philip's name. "Brand . . . ."

"Grant," Philip said. "Philip Grant."

"That's it," the cowboy said. "Philip Grant." A self-satisfied, know-it-all look crossed his face. "Channel 13, right?"

Philip smiled. "Six," he said.

"That's it," the cowboy said, his finger flipping through the air like a conductor's baton. "Philip Grant, Channel 6." He eyed Philip's bandage. "Looks like you took yourself a knock on the noggin." He turned to his partner, who'd obviously heard every word, elbowed him in the ribs, and said, "See that guy over there—that's Phil Grant from the Channel 6 news."

A surprised look crossed his face.

Philip shook his head and smiled at Rebecca. "It isn't easy being famous," he said.

Bright sunshine was already lighting the desert as Rebecca and Philip turned up the winding driveway that led to Benjamin Rutherford's home.

Rebecca glanced at the digital readout on the dashboard of Philip's car. "Right on time," she said as they pulled to a stop in front of his door.

Rutherford lived in a sprawling, split-level home in fashionable Fountain Hills, north of Phoenix. The landscaping was desert natural, and the acres that surrounded his home were as pristine as the remotest regions of a national park.

Rebecca took a minute to freshen up her makeup, using the mirror on the inside of the windshield visor. "We sure make a pretty couple,'' she noted, glancing at the stubble that peppered Philip's cheeks.

''Nothing that a few hours of sleep and a good shower won't cure,'' he said.

They stepped from the car and rang the bell.

To their surprise the door was opened almost immediately by Benjamin Rutherford, looking drawn and haggard in a pair of jeans and an orange-and-black cowboy shirt. His gray hair hung limply over his forehead, and he, too, was in need of a shave.

''What do you want?'' he asked brusquely.

''Sammi Stewart was arrested last night for assault with a deadly weapon,'' Philip said, dispensing with amenities. He glanced at Rebecca and added, ''She tried to kill us.''

''I heard.''

''Then maybe you've heard that she's being held on suspicion of murdering both the private investigator Cole hired to find Rebecca and the one you hired to keep Rebecca from being found.''

Rutherford's eyes narrowed suspiciously. ''What do you mean the one *I* hired?''

''Why don't we talk about it inside?'' Philip asked.

Rutherford ushered them grudgingly into a spacious living room. Monique Rutherford, her bleached hair a mess of fright-wig proportions, smoked quietly in a gold-leather wing-backed chair.

''I heard from Wendell last night,'' Philip said as he and Rebecca seated themselves on a long, comfortable sofa.

''Who didn't?'' Rutherford asked. ''He woke us up with a phone call in the middle of the night, begging me to help get his girlfriend off the hook. Asking me to use my influence.'' He snorted in disgust.

''Couldn't get back to sleep?'' Philip asked, surveying his disheveled condition.

Rutherford took a deep breath. ''We're a little anxious about this entire affair.''

''Not that it's any of your business,'' Monique added from behind a billowing cloud of tobacco smoke.

''Maybe it is, maybe it isn't,'' Philip said. ''Wendell didn't come around last night to ask me any favors. He showed up to tell me a story.''

''That boy's full of stories,'' Rutherford scoffed. ''You'd better be careful what you believe. I gave up on it years ago.''

Rebecca leveled her eyes on him. ''He told us that the two of you hired Pepper to keep me away from my inheritance.''

Rutherford was silent for a moment. His wife surveyed him coolly. ''If you had been in my place, you would have done the same thing,'' he said at last.

''Would we?'' Philip asked. ''You own a .38, don't you?''

''I own several guns.''

''I'm talking about a collector's piece given to you by your brother.''

Rutherford returned Philip's gaze. ''The Colt?'' he asked.

''You guessed it.''

''What are you getting at?'' Rutherford asked.

Philip leaned forward in his seat. Rebecca saw the thrill of the fight lighting his eyes. ''Do I have to paint a picture?'' he asked. ''Both the investigators were killed with a .38.''

Rutherford was suddenly on the defensive. ''There are millions of .38's out there,'' he said belligerently.

Philip laughed wryly and settled back into his seat. ''I suppose you're right. But how many matched pairs of Colts like yours are there? Your son has the other, doesn't he?''

Rutherford's eyes narrowed. ''That's right,'' he said cautiously.

''Did Wendell tell you that the gun Sammi fired at us this evening was the same one that was used in the murders of Pepper and Tipton?''

''He said she was being questioned about the murders,'' Rutherford stated. ''But he didn't mention any specifics.''

''Maybe not to you.''

Rutherford tried vainly to conceal his curiosity. ''Get on with it,'' he said.

''What time last night did Wendell call you for help?''

''It was almost three o'clock.''

Philip nodded. ''He started pounding on my door at around four. I guess that as soon as he finished with you, he decided to come to me.''

He paused and eyed Rutherford, then turned his attention on Monique. She was slouched in her seat, cigarette dangling from her lips, looking not at all glamorous. His gaze returned to Rutherford.

''Wendell says you're the killer.''

''Benjamin?'' Monique asked, suddenly sitting straight. A smile crossed her face. ''Why, that's absurd!''

Rutherford slumped back in his chair and crossed his arms over his chest, apparently relieved now that the accusation had been voiced. "Ridiculous," he said quietly.

"Wendell said he came by last night, just before the meeting with Cole. Is that right?"

"Of course, it's right," Rutherford said. "He came by to scream and shout about losing his inheritance and to help himself to some of our booze." He shook his head sadly. "The boy's been on a free ride for too long."

"You keep your gun collection in a row of glass cases, don't you, in the rec room?"

"What of it?"

"Wendell says that he exchanged his gun for yours last night, just before the meeting."

"What possible reason would he have for doing that?" Rutherford asked.

"To frame you for the murders of Pepper and Tipton."

The color drained from Rutherford's face. He swallowed several times. "I don't believe it," he finally managed to choke out.

Rather than slowing the pace of questioning, Philip increased the tempo. "He was afraid that Sammi had used his gun to commit the murders. He didn't want to see her go to jail, so he visited you last night, pretending to be worried about the will. His real purpose was to exchange his gun, the one he thought was a murder weapon, for yours."

"He wouldn't do that," Rutherford protested.

"You can imagine his surprise," Philip continued, "when he learned that the gun he had just picked out of your display case turned out to be the true murder weapon.''

''No,'' Rutherford said, ''no.''

''Believe it,'' Monique said, her tone cold and heartless. ''I told you to be careful of him.'' She turned to Philip. ''While he was storming around here last night, he swore that he would never let anyone take his money from him.''

''But you're his father,'' Rebecca said to Rutherford. ''Surely you intended to split your inheritance with him, to include him in the business.''

''No,'' Rutherford said, his voice almost a whisper. ''As far as I was concerned, Wendell was no longer a son of mine. He was spoiled rotten.''

He gazed at the ceiling and spoke quietly. ''It was my fault, I suppose. I catered to his every whim.'' He shook his head sadly. ''But it was over. I had explained to him in no uncertain terms that it was time he learned to act like a man and stand on his own two feet.'' He faced the carpet. ''I could never have expected it would turn out like this.

''I bought him everything he wanted,'' he continued. ''But I couldn't buy him a sense of pride. He never worked a day in his life, and I don't suppose he ever will unless he has to.'' He licked his lips and gazed at Rebecca. ''In a way, I was relieved when you were discovered,'' he said. ''It meant Wendell would be cut off at last, finally and forever, from the unending supply of money he was so accustomed to. It meant he would have to find a job and earn a living. I had hoped that it might mean he would find himself, at last, a sense of personal pride.''

''And look what it got you instead,'' Monique scoffed.

''Your own son, making up some ridiculous story about trading guns from your collection, trying to shift the suspicion for two murders onto your shoulders.''

Rutherford eyed his wife silently, then dejectedly dropped his face.

''Do you record the serial numbers of the weapons in your collection?'' Philip asked.

Rutherford shook his head slowly. ''No. I don't own a collection in the true sense of the word. I simply accumulate pieces that I find interesting or that are given to me. I own a number of weapons, but most of them are of little value to anyone other than myself.''

''The police are going to want to see the gun,'' Philip said. ''They'll want to run tests on it, examine it, search for any clues as to its true owner.''

Rutherford was silent.

''I'd like to see it,'' Philip said.

''Why?'' he snapped, his voice suddenly angry. ''What will seeing it prove?''

''You may be able to tell whether its position has been shifted.''

''I hardly think I'd notice something as inconsequential as that.''

Philip was silent for a moment. ''Is there any particular reason why you don't want me to see the gun?'' he asked.

''Haven't you already caused me enough trouble?'' Rutherford responded. ''Get out of my house.''

Philip stood his ground. ''This is all going to come out sooner or later. I'm giving you the chance to cooperate in a murder investigation. It won't look good if you refuse the offer.''

Rutherford glared at him momentarily, obviously weighing his options. "I suppose you're right," he said. He pushed himself from his seat and slicked his hair from his forehead. "But I still don't believe it. I can't believe Wendell would tell a story as malicious as this."

Philip offered no condolences, and he cut off Rebecca's with a sharp look.

"This way," Rutherford said, leading them from the room, leaving Monique alone to her cigarettes and private thoughts.

They walked down a long hallway that led to the rear of the house and entered the rec room.

"There they are," Rutherford said wearily, indicating a series of glass cases anchored to the far wall. Stuffed animal heads and mounted trophy fish were displayed here and there. A pool table sat in the center of the room.

The trio circled it and approached a case near the center of the display. "I keep the revolvers here," he explained. Numerous guns were propped in various positions inside the cases.

Suddenly Rutherford stopped, staring through the glass at a scattering of handguns. "I don't believe it," he said, sliding the glass door open.

"What is it?" Philip asked.

Rebecca's eyes scanned the interior of the case. She was amazed by the sheer number of firearms.

"It's missing," Rutherford said. "The Colt is missing."

She watched his face, not certain if his expression displayed true surprise or calculated deception.

Chapter Fourteen

Rebecca was beginning to feel like a fixture in the Channel 6 newsroom. She sat at Philip's desk, feeling self-conscious about her haggard appearance, and smiled good mornings to the faces she recognized. When she finally saw him making his way across the office, she could tell by the expression on his face that the meeting with Blanchard hadn't gone well.

The stubble of his beard cast a shadow over his face, and dark circles extended under his eyes. The bandage clinging to the side of his head only served to make him look more ragged. Neither of them had slept in over twenty-four hours, but the exhaustion he was feeling couldn't obscure the anger that burned brightly in his eyes.

"Let's get out of here," he said, gently guiding her from the station by the elbow.

They walked in silence to his car. Despite the early hour, shimmers of heat were already rising from the blacktop.

"It didn't go too well," he said when they'd reached his car. He pressed his hands against the top of the door frame and leaned his weight into his extended arms. He turned to look at her. "I think I'm going to be cut from the Antarctic deal," he said.

"How can they do that?" she asked, feeling guilty for the twinge of joy she felt. "I thought everything was set."

He stood straight and faced the big Channel 6 sign atop the station without really seeing it. "It was mine," he said. "Until my credibility came into question."

"How could anyone have doubts about your credibility?" she asked. "You've covered this story in an absolutely honest and straightforward manner."

He smiled wryly. "It's not the story," he explained, "but the way I handled it. Reporters must remain objective about what they're covering. Obviously I lost my objectivity when I decided to take this on as a favor for you."

"But you haven't changed any of the facts," Rebecca argued. "You've simply covered the story."

"That's the point," Philip said. "I shouldn't have covered it at all. I should have passed it off to someone else. We have plenty of good reporters working here. As it stands, when viewers learn that you're my girlfriend, they'll have a hard time believing anything I have to say about this case."

She noted his use of the word *girlfriend*. "How many people will really care about this?" she asked, ready to dismiss the entire event at the Purple Room as merely a curiosity that few would take particular interest in.

Rebecca thought she noted the faintest hint of despair in Philip's voice when he responded. "The *Informer* cared enough to run it as a front-page story. Blanchard made sure he read it to me. He even read the paragraph on the op-ed page that discussed the weaknesses and lack of integrity found in television journalists.'' He shook his head at the not-too-distant memory. ''Anyway,'' he said, ''it looks like Antarctica is out.'' He flashed her a weak grin. ''You might be glad to hear that.''

''Not if it makes you feel like this,'' she said sincerely. It wasn't fair, she thought, that something he had counted on for so long could be suddenly whisked so easily from under his feet. Knowing that she was the cause only compounded her feelings of guilt.

''You still have a chance of winning back your place on the Antarctic expedition,'' she said.

''Really? What's that?''

''Find out who really killed Tipton and Pepper. Get to the bottom of the story. Beat the police to the punch.''

''That could just end up getting me in deeper,'' he said. ''Blanchard pulled me from the story. He said he's going to assign someone else to it.''

The resignation in his voice sparked Rebecca's temper. ''So you just plan to give up, then?''

''My hands are tied. I've already lost the Antarctic deal. I can't afford to risk anything else.''

''You can't afford not to risk anything else. I know you, Philip Grant. You wouldn't be able to face yourself in the mirror every morning if you let this slip away. You had better make your decision right now. Either you're going to stand here in this parking lot feeling sorry for yourself, or you're going to do what you've always done: Fight your way out.''

She faced him with her hands on her hips, anger and indignation smoldering in her expression.

Suddenly Philip smiled. "So you want me to come out swinging, huh?"

"If you don't solve this, someone else will," she said, her tone softening. "You'll receive absolutely no credit for all the work you've done so far."

"All the work *we've* done," he corrected. He circled the car and opened her door. "Come on," he said. "We've got a date with Wendell Rutherford."

It was nine-thirty by the time Rebecca and Philip arrived at Wendell's patio home in an exclusive section of Scottsdale. His white Porsche was parked in the carport.

He answered the door dressed in a pair of baggy, blue walking shorts and a T-shirt and led them into a small living room crammed with expensive stereo equipment. Furniture was sparse, but what there was was obviously of high quality. On the walls were hung a variety of bizarre and macabre paintings, mostly done in shades of black and purple. Rebecca wasn't surprised to spot Sammi's name scrawled in red in the bottom corner of one.

"What do you mean the gun was missing?" Wendell cried when Philip gave him the information. "I told you I put it right there in the cabinet."

Philip eyed Wendell speculatively.

"Why would I lie about something like that?" he asked, noting Philip's gaze and remembering the punch his fist packed.

"I didn't say you were lying. I'm simply stating the facts."

"Why would they take the gun?" Wendell asked, mostly to himself.

"There's no reason for it, is there?"

The air conditioner clicked on, and Rebecca shivered as a wave of cold air washed over her.

For a moment Wendell looked as if he was about to fly into one of his rages, but he changed his mind and remained silent.

"The fact is," Philip continued, "you've already admitted to stealing your father's gun. Now yours is missing. Why should we suspect that your father has it? Until we visited him last night and told him about the switch you'd made, he had no reason to suspect anything was amiss with his collection."

Wendell snapped his fingers. "That's it," he said. "He knew that the murder weapon was in his collection. He also knew that the police would be investigating anyone concerned with my uncle's will. He probably pulled the gun from his collection and got rid of it in the desert."

"It seems to me that you're grasping for straws," Philip said. "Your whole story sounded cockeyed from the beginning. You seem to have too many ready-made explanations. But explanations don't change facts: You're the only one we know for sure who has handled both the guns."

Wendell jumped from his seat. "Are you saying I'm the killer?" he shouted.

"You'd better remember what happened the last time you jumped like that," Philip cautioned. "I'm in no mood to play your games today."

He settled back into his seat, a gloomy expression on his face. "I didn't do it," he protested weakly.

"Unless we can get your father to lead us to your gun,

I'm afraid I'm going to have to believe otherwise,'' Philip said. ''I think the police will too. We're headed over there right now.''

''You can't do that,'' Wendell protested. ''They'll throw me in jail.''

Philip stood. ''That's where killers belong.'' He took Rebecca's hand, and they left.

The interior of the car was already hot, despite the early hour. Philip switched on the air conditioner. ''Now to see what he does,'' he said.

They circled the block once, returned, and parked half a block from Wendell's house.

''If I know Wendell like I think I know Wendell, we won't be here long,'' Philip said.

''I thought we were headed for the police department,'' Rebecca said.

''Just a bluff. You said it yourself—I've got to beat the police on this one. Giving them all the information we've managed to piece together is hardly going to put us in the lead.'' He watched Wendell's home through the windshield. ''My bet is he'll storm around his house for a few minutes, trying to decide what he should do, then he'll head out to his father's place to butt heads.''

''Why would he do that if he's the killer?'' Rebecca asked.

''If he *were* the killer and he knew where the guns were, he wouldn't,'' Philip responded. ''But I'm beginning to think that Wendell really is telling the truth.''

''I hate to say I told you so.''

''Yes, you did. And I'm glad to know that you hated to remind me of that fact.''

Suddenly Wendell raced from his front door and jumped into his car. The engine roared to life, and he backed into the street with a squeal of rubber. With another squeal he shot off down the road.

"What did I tell you?" Philip asked, accelerating from the curb. "We're never going to keep up with him once he hits those rural roads, but at least we know where he's going."

As Philip had predicted, Wendell's Porsche was parked on the drive in front of Benjamin Rutherford's home. The drapes on the front windows were drawn tightly. Philip pulled in behind Wendell and killed the engine.

"What now?" Rebecca asked.

"We wait. They're going to have a showdown in there. If Wendell is telling the truth, Rutherford will know that lying about the whereabouts of the gun will get him nowhere. He'll have to make some kind of a deal. I imagine that Wendell would settle for cash."

Rebecca shook her head. "I can't believe this family."

"It's a family in name only. Wendell obviously hates his father. He tried to set him up to take the rap for two murders. Now he's going to blackmail him." He smiled wryly. "When he comes out, he'll think I've got something on him. He'll wonder why I followed him out here. That will scare him. Then I'll remind him how Sammi is suffering behind bars. We'll have the truth soon enough."

"But what if Wendell is lying?" Rebecca asked. "What if he never really switched the guns?"

"If he hadn't switched them, he wouldn't be here

trying to find out what had happened to the one that's missing. I'm convinced that Benjamin Rutherford is our man. And as soon as Wendell shows his face, I'm going to jump on him and get the information I need to put Rutherford behind bars for murder."

Rebecca listened, feeling certain that Philip was correct.

Suddenly a woman screamed from inside the house. A gunshot cracked, followed quickly by another, and glass crashed as the living-room window shattered.

"Get down!" Philip ordered, shoving Rebecca down into the safety of her seat.

Through the confusion she heard Wendell calling, "I'm hit, I'm hit." His plaintive wail rang clearly through the broken glass of the window. "He shot me."

"I'm going in for a look," Philip said, dashing from the car.

Without thinking twice, Rebecca jumped from her seat and followed him.

They ran through the front door and turned into the living room.

Wendell lay on the floor, grasping his thigh. Monique Rutherford was on her knees beside him, attempting to get a look at the wound through his interlocked fingers.

"He tried to kill me, he tried to kill me," he cried over and over. "Don't let him shoot me again. Please, please, don't let him shoot me."

Benjamin Rutherford stood beside the sofa, phone in hand. Rebecca spotted a small, chromed automatic on the end table. His gaze followed hers; then he spoke calmly into the receiver, his eyes locked on moaning

Wendell. ''Please send the police and an ambulance. There's been a shooting.'' He recited his address and hung up.

Philip dropped to his knees beside Wendell, joining Monique on the floor. ''Let's see it,'' he ordered, prying Wendell's fingers from the wound. He rolled his eyes with dismay. ''It's just a flesh wound,'' he said derisively. ''Barely a nick.''

Wendell glanced down at the wound, then closed his eyes. ''It's bleeding,'' he whined. ''He could have killed me.''

''Maybe if he'd had a feather,'' Philip said, standing. He faced Rutherford. ''What happened?''

''I didn't have a choice,'' Rutherford said.

Rebecca suddenly noticed the ashen tint to his face.

''He threatened me—attacked me with this.'' He displayed a painter's knife. ''He accused me of throwing away his pistol. When I denied it, he became enraged. He said I'd pay one way or another. He lunged at me.'' Rutherford struggled for breath and wiped his brow.

Monique knelt beside the ailing Wendell, crying softly, obviously shaken by the incident.

''You could have cut my artery, Dad,'' Wendell moaned. He continued to grip his leg as if he were dying.

Rebecca felt as though she were watching a scene from a bad movie. Wendell didn't seem to realize or care that he'd just forced his father to shoot at him. ''This better not get gangrene,'' he said.

Philip shook his head and escorted Rebecca back to the car. ''This is one gamble that didn't pay off. When

Blanchard finds out I didn't drop the case, he'll probably fire me.''

''What do we do now?'' Rebecca asked, leaning against the warm metal of the car body, suddenly overcome with exhaustion.

''What else? We wait for the police.''

Rebecca sighed deeply and leaned her head against Philip's chest. She felt herself drifting off to sleep beside him on the sofa.

They had been allowed to give their statements at the scene, then had returned to Philip's apartment. Both Wendell and Benjamin had been taken to the station for further questioning regarding the murders of Tipton and Pepper.

''I think I'll wait for them to call me,'' Philip said, referring to the station. ''Blanchard is bound to find out about our visit to the Rutherfords, and when he does, I can just about guarantee that my time with Channel 6 will be all but over.''

''I'm sorry,'' Rebecca said.

He smiled. ''Don't be. I've enjoyed all the excitement. I can't say I'm crazy about having to go hunting for a new job, though.'' He shrugged resignedly. ''I just wish we had been able to sort everything out. We still can't be sure who killed Pepper and Tipton. I guess the police will wind up getting the credit, after all.''

''Maybe you should call them before they call you,'' Rebecca suggested.

Philip closed his eyes. ''Maybe I should,'' he agreed. His hand stroked her hair. ''Maybe I will when I wake up.''

Rebecca settled deeply against his body. "Are you as tired as I am?"

He muttered something she couldn't understand, and his hand slid loosely around her shoulders. Exhaustion washed over her like a warm river. Things would work out for the best, she thought. They always did. She closed her eyes and fell asleep.

It seemed as though only minutes had passed before Rebecca was suddenly jolted out of a deep sleep.

Philip was straight in his seat, rubbing his eyes. "Someone's ringing the doorbell," he said.

Rebecca forced herself to sit up. "I didn't hear anything."

He glanced at his watch. "Three o'clock."

A hammering sounded at the door.

"Did you hear it that time?" he asked.

"I must have been dead to the world." She rubbed her cheeks and pushed the hair from her face.

"I think we both were." Philip crossed to the front door. Rebecca watched over her shoulder as he answered it.

"Thank goodness you're home," she heard a woman say. She recognized the voice as Monique Rutherford's.

"I'm sorry it took so long," Philip said. "We were just trying to catch a little sleep."

"I really must talk with you," Monique insisted. She stepped around Philip into the foyer. Her hair had been painstakingly styled, and she was wearing a light-pink summer dress. "It's about Tipton and Pepper."

"If you have anything to say regarding the murders,

I suggest you tell it to the police,'' Philip said. ''I'm no longer covering the story.''

''But you must,'' Monique implored. ''I want the story out. I can't live with it any longer.'' She turned her face to the side and sniffed quietly.

Philip closed the door and led her into the living room. ''I can't guarantee anything,'' he said. ''I'll listen to what you have to say and make my decisions from there.''

''But I want it out in the open,'' Monique persisted, settling into a chair, her purse on her lap. ''I want the truth to be told. That's why I came to you.'' She reached into her purse for a tissue. ''The police questioned Benjamin for several hours today. He was only just released.'' Suddenly she burst into tears. ''He didn't mean for it to end up this way.''

Rebecca approached Mrs. Rutherford and laid a comforting hand on her shoulder.

Monique gripped her hand. ''I'll be all right,'' she said. ''But Benjamin. . . .'' Her voice trailed off.

''What about Benjamin?'' Philip asked gently.

She dabbed her eyes with the tissue. ''He was only thinking of me. Of my future.''

''I understand that,'' Philip said.

''Tell me you believe me.''

''I believe you,'' he said quietly.

She pressed her eyes closed tightly. ''We all decided to hire Pepper to ensure that Jefferson Rutherford's daughter would never learn about her inheritance. I wish now that we had simply let events take their course. Everything would have been so much simpler.''

Her entire body trembled as she struggled to gain control of her emotions. "I never expected him to kill those two men." She broke into another round of sobs.

"Your husband killed them?" Philip asked.

She nodded quickly several times. "Pepper called him and said he thought that Tipton was about to make contact with Jefferson Rutherford's daughter. Benjamin drove to LA as soon as he hung up. He didn't fly, because he was afraid that a check of airline records would prove that he had traveled to LA, and he didn't want anyone to know that he was meddling with the conditions of the will." She paused for a moment. "He told me that he was going to try to make a deal with Tipton.

"Pepper had given him the name of the motel, and Benjamin drove there directly. Tipton, of course, knew my husband, and let him into the room. Benjamin tried to buy him off, but Tipton couldn't be persuaded. That's when . . . that's when it happened." She buried her face in her hands for several seconds.

"Pepper saw it all," she said at last. "Benjamin hadn't anticipated Pepper's surveillance." She wiped her eyes. "Pepper started to blackmail him. He said he had photographs of Benjamin entering the room."

She pulled a pack of cigarettes from her purse and lit one quietly. "Pepper ordered my husband to meet him at the irrigation canal. He told him to bring fifty thousand dollars." Her voice was shaky.

The cigarette trembled in Monique's fingers as she inhaled. "Benjamin went to the meeting. He didn't bring the money. He was going to try to stall Pepper along. The only thing he brought was his gun.

"There was a fight of some sort, and . . . and. . . ."

She turned away in tears. ''After Pepper was gone,'' she continued at last, ''Benjamin panicked. He wanted to hide the body where it wouldn't be found for several hours. He needed the time to think, he said. He started Pepper's car, put it into gear, and let it roll down into the canal. It flipped when it hit the concrete bank. He knew it wouldn't be spotted from the road.''

A heavy cloak of silence descended over the room. Monique avoided meeting their gaze.

''I'm sorry,'' she said suddenly, glancing from her cigarette to the coffee table. ''Do you have an ashtray?''

''Just a minute,'' Philip said. He disappeared into the kitchen and returned momentarily with a saucer, which he set before her.

''He had to do it, don't you see?'' Her eyes begged them to understand, and Rebecca noticed a hardness that she had not seen earlier. ''The fifty thousand was only a first payment. Pepper would have bled us dry.'' She snubbed the barely smoked cigarette in the saucer. Traces of her pink lipstick shone on the white paper.

Rebecca returned to the sofa, unable to shake the feeling that Monique was hiding something.

Philip regarded Mrs. Rutherford thoughtfully, pinching his lip. ''When it was all over,'' he said, ''your husband put the gun back into the case?''

She nodded.

''Strange for him to do so,'' he commented. ''He must have known that he would be a prime suspect and that his guns would probably be checked.''

''I don't know what he was thinking,'' Monique said,

a solitary tear tracing a path over her cheek. "Maybe he wasn't thinking at all."

"Why have you suddenly decided to come forward?" Philip asked.

"You were there this morning," she answered. "Benjamin shot his own son. Do you really have to ask me why?"

"I'm sorry," he said.

Rebecca watched Monique. Suddenly she wasn't at all sure that Mrs. Rutherford was telling the complete truth. Her tears somehow didn't seem natural, and there were too many of them. "Do you have any evidence to support all this?" she asked. From the corner of her eye she caught Philip's sharp look.

"The other gun," Monique said. "The one Wendell put in the display case. It's in my car." She stopped for a moment and bit her lip. "I also have a tape."

"What kind of tape?" Philip asked.

She slumped forward, unable to face either of them. "A cassette tape Benjamin made. He was carrying a small tape recorder when he went to meet with Pepper. He recorded the entire conversation." She paused. "He was hoping that he could somehow turn the tables on him. Everything's on it. The fight . . . the gunshot." Another rush of tears forced her to stop.

"Where are the gun and the tape?" Philip asked.

"I brought them with me. It's all in the car."

"I'm going to want to see them. Where are you parked?"

"Wendell gave me your address, but I wasn't sure which unit was yours, so I parked out by the office."

She fished for a key in her purse. ''Could you get it for me? It's the silver Jag. Everything is under the passenger seat.''

''I'll be back in a couple of minutes,'' Philip said.

Rebecca could read the excitement in his eyes. Finding the evidence would mean that his job was saved. He hurried out the door.

Rebecca turned her attention toward Monique, who was still quietly crying, her eyes on the floor.

''Is there anything I can get for you?'' she asked.

Monique sniffed and shook her head. She reached for her purse on the coffee table.

''Anything at all?'' Rebecca asked.

Suddenly Monique was no longer crying. Their eyes met. Hers were as hard and flat as a sheet of steel. ''He'll find the tape,'' she said, ''but it will be blank. He'll find the gun, too, but it won't be Wendell's.'' An evil grin split her face. ''Because I've got Wendell's right here.'' She snatched a revolver from the purse and leveled it on Rebecca. ''Get up,'' she ordered. ''Get into the kitchen. Now!''

Rebecca stood slowly. Monique motioned toward the kitchen with the pistol barrel. ''Hurry up,'' she said.

''What? Why? Why are you doing this?'' Rebecca asked, backing slowly across the carpet to the kitchen.

''As if you don't know,'' Monique said with a sneer. She reached into her purse and withdrew something wrapped in blue paper towel. ''You loused everything up.''

''What are you going to do?''

''Ask Pepper or Tipton.''

Rebecca's throat constricted. She couldn't breathe. "You won't get away with this."

"I think I will."

Slowly Rebecca backed into the kitchen. The soft carpet gave way to hard tile under her feet. Monique followed.

"It's mine," she said. "The money is mine. I earned it. I married Benjamin Rutherford, not you. How dare you think you can suddenly show up and steal what's mine?"

The gun trembled in Monique's hand. Her finger curled around the trigger. Rebecca's mouth was dry. "They'll know it's you," she said, playing for time, hoping to somehow stall Monique long enough for Philip to return.

"No," Monique said, "no, they won't, because I was kind enough to visit Wendell today after the police finished with him, and I helped change his bandage."

With her free hand she opened the blue paper towel, and displayed a bloodstained square of gauze. "He never could take care of himself," she sneered. "They'll find this when they find you."

"What about Philip?" Rebecca asked, trying to fight the panic that threatened to overpower her at any second.

"They'll find him too." Monique drew her lips up over her teeth in a savage smile. "Wendell's bandage, Wendell's gun. Wendell will go to jail, not me."

Philip's voice answered. "You're wrong, Monique." He stepped quickly around the corner from the living room.

Monique whirled on him. He stepped forward and captured her arm before she was able to draw a bead. With a quick movement he stripped the gun from her hand.

Monique faced him, paralyzed for a moment, then slowly sank to the floor.

"Are you all right?" he asked Rebecca.

She hadn't realized that she'd been holding her breath. "You couldn't have made it out to the office and back so quickly," she said, breathing heavily.

Philip watched Monique. She was on her knees, holding her head in her hands. "I never left the front porch," he said. "I thought it was strange that she would ask me to leave. I watched as best as I could through the pebbled glass, and when I saw you two suddenly walking for the kitchen, I remembered something you'd told me about the murder scene in Tipton's room."

Monique began weeping loudly. This time, Rebecca thought, her tears seemed sincere.

"Cigarette butts," Philip said. "Smeared with lipstick." He nodded his head toward the living room. "Just like the one out there in the saucer."

Monique was sobbing on the floor. "I didn't do anything wrong," she said. "I didn't do anything." She looked to Philip, then Rebecca. "All I wanted was the money. Just the money." She buried her face in her hands. "Is there anything wrong with wanting money?"

"Only when you commit murder to get it," Philip said.

Chapter Fifteen

Sunlight filled Cole's office, shining off the dark woodwork and lighting the spines of the blue-leather bound law journals that lined his bookcases.

He handed a sheaf of official-looking documents across his desk to Rebecca. "These are copies of the original adoption papers, which we recovered from both Nevada and Arizona."

She thumbed quickly through the forms, noting a variety of stamps, seals, and signatures.

"Because this action involved only your father, your mother's name has been blacked out," he added. "You'll also find signed affidavits from both Benjamin and Wendell Rutherford stating that they will not contest your status as heir, thereby allowing you to inherit under the conditions stipulated in the will."

Rebecca glanced at Philip. He smiled at her. "Congratulations," he said. "You're a millionaire."

"Not quite yet," Cole cautioned. He handed her another stack of forms. "You'll need to sign these first."

She scanned them briefly.

"They're tax forms and transfers of ownership for Jefferson Rutherford's various holdings," Cole said. "You need not sign them now. In fact, I would recommend that you not sign them until you've had an attorney look them over.'' He smiled. ''Although, I understand that you've had quite a bit of experience yourself with legal documents over the past several weeks.''

She grinned. The statements and depositions in police squad rooms were a thing of the past now. Of course, she would still have to testify at the trials of Sammi Stewart and Monique Rutherford.

''I told her that she should take some of that money and go to law school,'' Philip said. In the four weeks since the shooting at the Purple Room, his hair had grown in fully enough to cover the small scar left by Sammi's bullet.

''Law school might not be a bad investment,'' Cole agreed. ''You might try something in finance as well.''

Rebecca grimaced. ''I've been thinking about it. Unfortunately, I've already had two years of business school, and I didn't much care for it.''

Cole smiled. ''I think managing your own fortune will be more interesting than anything the textbooks might offer.''

''I could always pay someone to take care of it,'' she said with a laugh.

''You had better be careful who you hire,'' Cole cautioned. ''The world is full of Monique Rutherfords, just waiting to take advantage of anyone who will let them get one foot in the door.''

She thought of Benjamin Rutherford, alone now, duped by the beauty of a wife too young, and destroyed by the actions of a son whose love money could not buy.

''What will happen to Benjamin?'' she asked.

''He'll have to come to grips with himself,'' Cole said,

and Rebecca noted the sadness in his voice. ''I expect that you'll get to know him fairly well,'' he added. ''You'll be partners, of course. He drives a hard deal. You could learn a lot from him.''

''I think I already have,'' she said.

''What about Wendell?'' Philip asked. ''Will he face charges for switching guns?''

Cole shook his head. ''No. At the time Wendell made the switch, he had no sure knowledge that a crime had been committed with his gun. In fact, none had. I suppose his father could file charges for theft, but I doubt if that's likely.''

''You know them better than we do,'' Rebecca said. ''Do you suppose that they'll ever get back together?''

Cole spread his hands face up on his desk. ''Stranger things have happened.'' He eyed them both. ''And what about you two? What plans do you have?''

Rebecca suddenly felt awkward. The phrasing of the question somehow seemed to imply a continuing relationship between them. A relationship, she knew, that was not to be.

''Well,'' she said, ''Philip will be traveling to Antarctica for a year to work on a documentary with some professors from the University of Arizona.'' She forced the smile to remain on her face. ''And me,'' she said, ''I suppose that I'll move out here and begin taking control of my new businesses.''

''Teaching is out of the picture for a while, I would imagine,'' Cole said.

''For the time being. I called Vance Foster last night to tell him I wouldn't be coming back.''

"Vance is your principal?" Cole asked.

She nodded. "The call was just a formality, really. Vance and I are close friends. He hadn't expected me to return."

Cole smiled. "Did he have any words of advice?"

"As a matter of fact," Rebecca said with a laugh, "he asked for a loan."

"You should begin expecting a lot of that."

"He was just kidding, of course. But he's always been there when I needed him." She cocked her head to the side. "As far as I'm concerned, he can have anything he wants."

"Uh-oh," Philip said. "I think we're dealing with a soft touch here."

Cole grinned. "I wouldn't be so sure." He stood from his desk. "My secretary is holding something for you. If you'll excuse me, I'll be back in a moment." He left the office.

Rebecca looked at Philip and grinned. Ever since he had accepted the position in Antarctica, one day after Monique's arrest, Rebecca had felt the need to force her good spirits when she was around him. She had even tried not seeing him as often as she'd wanted, as if a gradual withdrawal would somehow make his inevitable departure somehow easier.

He smiled back at her.

Cole returned, carrying a white envelope. "Jefferson Rutherford left this with his will," he said. "He left instructions that, should his daughter be found, it be given to her."

Rebecca turned the envelope in her hands. The words

To my daughter were etched on the front in bold, black handwriting. ''What is it?'' she asked.

''He never told me,'' Cole said.

Rebecca slid her finger under the flap and tore the envelope open. Inside were two sheets of paper. She unfolded one of them. ''It's a note,'' she said. She scanned it briefly, then read it aloud.

''To the daughter I never knew. May you never make the mistake I made. Follow your heart, and you'll be happy always.''

She glanced from Cole to Philip. Both men were silent. She set the note on the desk and opened the second sheet. She drew her breath in sharply.

''What does it say?'' Philip asked.

''It's a contract,'' Rebecca said. She turned to Cole. ''The one you drew up before I was born.'' She read it quickly, then handed it to Cole.

''Yes,'' he confirmed, ''this is the contract.''

She looked to Philip. ''My mother's name,'' she said, ''is Mary O'Bannion.''

Philip smiled at her. ''Now you know. At last.''

Her eyes filled with tears, and she averted her gaze.

''Do you think we could be alone for a minute?'' she heard Philip ask.

''Certainly.''

She wiped the tears from her cheeks as Cole left.

''I feel like such a fool,'' she said. ''I don't know why I'm crying.''

Philip was beside her, pulling her to her feet. He held her hand, and they walked to one of the windows that overlooked the city. A blue sky spread endlessly before them.

"I'm not going," he said.

"What?"

"I'm not going to Antarctica."

"But you've given them your word."

He scoffed. "They were ready to fire me a few weeks ago. I guess Jefferson Rutherford makes sense to me."

Rebecca couldn't believe what she was hearing. "You're going to stay?" she asked.

He circled his arms around her and pulled her close. "I couldn't very well leave you alone to all those evil people Cole was warning you about." He smiled. "And if you run into as much trouble looking for your mother as you did your father. . . ." He smiled at her.

"You know me pretty well, don't you?"

He touched his forehead lightly to hers. "I know you'll want someone to celebrate St. Patrick's Day with."

She kissed him, then, and he held her tightly. So tightly, she knew, that he would never let her go.